VINCENT W. FAIELLA

MILTON & HUGO L.L.C.
4407 Park Ave., Suite 5
Union City, NJ 07087, USA

Website: *www. miltonandhugo.com*
Hotline: *1- 888-778-0033*
Email: *info@miltonandhugo.com*

Ordering Information:
Quantity sales. Special discounts are granted to corporations, associations, and other organizations. For more information on these discounts, please reach out to the publisher using the contact information provided above.

Library of Congress Control Number:	2024903411	
ISBN-13:	979-8-89285-040-7	[Paperback Edition]
	979-8-89285-041-4	[Digital Edition]

Rev. date: 02/14/2024

Written by:

Vincent W. Faiella

Illustrated by:

Contents

Acknowledgments

I would like to first thank my family and
closest friends for continually
supporting me in this endeavor. If it hadn't been for those
treasured individuals, my life would have been greatly burdened
with a heavy weight and prevented me from a happy, enriched life.
Secondly, I would like to dedicate this collection of short stories,
the first of my published works, to the illustrators that
agreed to create such awe-inspiring pieces for my stories.
They have made my dream a reality, and it goes
without saying, I wouldn't have made it this far
without their faith and contribution in my work.
And lastly, I would like to contribute this publication to those
who have kept the traditions of Halloween through their
own work such as Michael Dougherty and Alvin Schwartz
who have inspired me since adolescences to carry on
the spirit. They, among others, are true masters
of horror and story-telling that I can only
hope I become in the years to come.

Introduction

In my life, leading up to the creation of this book, I had often heard from others that Halloween isn't a 'real' holiday or that it was a creation of candy-companies to endorse their wares. Before you read these short-stories, I (as the author) felt it necessary to dispel those misinformed, absent-minded thinking by revealing the long history of Halloween as it came into the new world...

Samhain (/ˈsɑːwɪn, ˈsaʊɪn/; Irish: [ˈsˠəuɪnʲ] Scottish Gaelic: [ˈs̪ãũ.ɪɲ]) is a Gaelic festival marking the end of the harvest season and the beginning of the winter season (or the "darker half") of the year. In the northern hemisphere, it begins on November 1st, but the celebrations begin on October 31st, which the Celtic day begins and ends at sunset. This festival was in the middle of the autumn equinox and winter solstice. It is also one of the four Gaelic seasonal festivals, Imbolc, Beltaine, and the Lughnasa. Historically, it spread throughout Ireland, Scotland, and the Isle of Man (or "Sauin"). A similar festival held by the Brittonic Celts, called "Calan Gaeaf" in Wales, "Kalan Gwav" in Cornwall, and "Kala Goañv" in Brittany.

Samhain had believed to have Celtic pagan origins, and some Neolithic passage tombs in Ireland aligned with the sunrise at the time of Samhain. It is first mentioned in the earliest Irish literature, from the 9th century, and is associated with many important events in Irish mythology. The earliest literature says that Samhain marked the great gatherings and feasts, and when the ancient burial mounds were open, locals believed them to be portals to the Otherworld. The Otherworld describes a paradisal fairyland or spirit land rather than a scary place, the realm of the deities and dead of everlasting youth, beauty, health, abundance, and joy. The Otherworld in the idea of Celtic people became hard to distinguish and sometimes overlapped with the Christian idea of hell or heaven as this was often an analogy made to the Celtic idea of an otherworld or Scandinavian idea of a world tree. Some of the literature also associates Samhain with bonfires and sacrifices.

The festival of Samhain did NOT get recorded in detail until the early modern era. Like Beltaine, special bonfires were lit, deemed to have protective and cleansing powers, accompanied by rituals to invoke these powers. Furthermore, Samhain was a liminal (or 'threshold' festival) when the boundaries between the world and the Otherworld were thinnest, meaning that Aos Sí (the 'spirits' or 'fairies') could easily come into the world of the living than before; most scholars see the Aos Sí as remnants of pagan gods. For example, offerings of food and drink were made during Samhain to appease these gods to ensure the survival of people and livestock during the coming winter. Some thought that the souls of their dead ancestors would revisit their homes seeking hospitality, and a place was set at the table for them during a Samhain meal. This is similar to how the Mexican culture celebrated día de Los Muertos (or "Day of the Dead"). Mumming (or "guising") was a part of the festival from at least the early-modern era, whereby people went door-to-door in costumes, reciting verses in exchange for food. The costumes may have been a way of imitating or scaring the Aos Sí by disguises.

In the 9th century, the Christian Church had shifted All Saint's Day to November 1st, while November 2nd became All Souls' Day later. Over time, some believed that Samhain and All Saints' Day plus All Souls' Day influenced each other and 3eventually merged into the modern Halloween that we've come to celebrate today. This theorized to be the result of Scottish and Irish immigrants coming into America during the 1700s. This movement did not commercialize until the 1900s, when postcards and die-cut paper decorations were produced and sold in stores. It progressed to Halloween costumes appearing in stores during the 1930s and 'trick-or-treating' customs in the 1950s. Some folklorists have used the name 'Samhain' to refer to Gaelic 'Halloween' traditions until the 19th century.

Notably, Christmas was founded upon the same principles, whereas it had immigrated from different parts of the world and cultures, reformulated by the Christian. Originally, it was known as Yuletide, which was a festival historically observed by the Germanic people. Scholars have connected the original celebration of Yule to the Wild Hunt, the god Odin, and the pagan Anglo-Saxon Mōdraniht. Pagans and paganism (from classical Latin pāgānus "rural," "rustic," later "civilian") were found in the 4th century by early Christians for people in the Roman Empire who practiced polytheism; the practice of worshipping multiple gods and goddesses. The pagans founded their belief upon honoring nature itself rather than a divine, abstract entity. Pagans and paganism often faced accusations of witchcraft and devil-worshipping as persecution by other religions and cultures. Specifically, the Roman god Pan was confused for a satanic symbol due to his beastly nature and goat appearance (hooves, horns, hair, etc.). They regarded these ritual sacrifices as an integral part of ancient Graeco-Roman religion and indicated whether a person was a pagan or Christian in the end.

People commonly celebrated Yuletide to welcome the winter solstice, the time when the seasons would become colder, the days grow longer, and the nights shorter. It was a pagan holiday that gave thanks to the harvest and rejoices in the new year. This holiday would later depart from its pagan roots and undergo the Christianized reformulation, the adaptation of non-Christian elements of culture or historical facts to the worldview of Christianity, which resulted in the term Christmastide. This was a common practice applied to the recasting of religious and cultural activities, beliefs, and imageries of "pagan" peoples into a Christianized form as a strategy for Christianization. Furthermore, many present-day Christmas customs and traditions such as the Yule log, a specially selected log burnt on a hearth as a Christmas tradition.

Another tradition was the Yule goat, a Scandinavian and Northern European Yule, and Christmas symbol and tradition. Many theories branch from different areas but typically contributed towards the last sheaf of grain bundled in the harvest, accredited with magical properties as the spirit of the harvest and saved for the Yule celebrations and thus to the Yule goat (julbocken). A man dressed similarly to Saint Nicholas or Santa Claus would accompany the Yule goat as well. The Yule boar, the boar sacrificed as part of the celebration of Yule in Germanic paganism, on whose bristles practitioners made solemn vows, a tradition is known as heitstrenging, was known for the creation of the Christmas ham. Finally, Yule singing, the practice of people going door-to-door, singing and offering a drink from the wassail bowl (a cider infused with citrus fruit slices and cinnamon sticks) in exchange for gifts (known as caroling). These examples and others stem from pagan Yule traditions. These terms with an etymological equivalent to Yule are still used in Nordic countries and Estonia to describe Christmas and other festivals occurring during the winter holiday season.

To end on a personal note, I hope this brief background account has established stronger connection to the stories and the spirit of Samhain or Halloween as we know it now. For those of Celtic descent, I implore you to respect these traditions and the supernatural wonder of Samhain. And for those who are without such lineage, I hope that you will consider taking Halloween in better light rather than having it dismissed for another commercialized holiday.

With that said, let's begin with our first night...

October 19th

The Cat

Within Salem, Massachusetts, there is an unfamiliar, unnamed town surrounded by the secluded mountain range within an ever-expanding forest under a starry night. For the time being, it will simply be known as the Town. There were local shops, restaurants, bakeries, post offices, and stores with a homestead feeling to its neighborhood. The winters were cold, the springs were warm, the summers were hot, but the fall seasons were just suitable for the Town. There'd be a sweet-sour crisp smell as a cool breeze swept the baked leaves into the air. The leaves would twirl in whirlwinds of colors, a mix of red, yellow, orange, and brown watercolors, traveling across the blackened roads.

As the trail of leaves brushed past the streets, you see an alley between a local butcher shop and a farmer's market store. The two buildings share the passage where they dispose of their garbage in the dumpsters and accompanying trashcans. These alleys are usually kept relatively clean, with only a few scraps of debris and crumpled wads of paper left behind the nearby trashcans. On one such trashcan was a small black cat, sleeping on its lid. Its fur was well-kept and clean, a completely black slick coat with an unusual collar of goldish yellow fur around its neck. It was not your normal alley-cat. She seemed out of place, and yet she had remained unnamed herself for a long time.

Awaking from her slumber, she stretched her arms and unclenched her paws, revealing a row of sharp, yellowish claws. She shook her head briskly and leaped to the concrete pavement with a gentle landing. The cold night breeze made her quiver, and so she trailed along the brick wall of the butcher shop to shield herself from the opposing wind. As she came across the edge to where the sidewalk met the black-paved

1

road, she looked outward to the other side to where the rest of the neighborhood resided. There were medium-sized houses lined up near each other, blending around the curve of the sidewalk. Each house had a different shape that contained a distinctive quality that separated them all rather than incorporating them like carbon copies of each other. The cat approached the crosswalk leading to the neighborhood in hopes of reaching the house on the corner.

She hadn't had any food all day, the sun had set, and the night would become colder. She would either die of the cold or die from starvation; either was an unpleasant thought. The butcher shop and farmer's market were closed, and they hadn't left any scraps for her to salvage from their trashcans. Her only available resource was Thomas Cabal.

His house was littered with unlit, uncarved pumpkins on the porch, varying in sizes, shapes, and colors, preparing for the upcoming Halloween season. Thomas had always celebrated Halloween with an unmatched spirit over any other holiday. Thus, it became a popular house for trick-or-treaters, especially as it was a reasonably large house in a dark, old Victorian stylized build. The wooden walls were freshly painted brown, and a black tiled roof with grayish window panels with tinted glass. Along with the blood-orange-colored door, it had a brass knocker with the head of a furious lion, the house surrounded by shrubs of wilted lilies around the front porch, dying from an early case of frost. This was a household that celebrated the holiday of Halloween with good, frightful cheer.

Thomas Cabal, a local newspaper editor, was a strange and shy man that kept to himself. He kept himself busy writing stories with hopes of publication that took most of his time; no time to socialize with other human beings. At the same time, however, he seems ill-confident in his ability, questioning what others may think of his writing. This had caused him to delve into procrastination, mountains of paper filling his office that longed to be born into a full-fledged book. On many long nights, she had patrolled the neighborhood for any offerings out of charity from neighbors, and only Cabal did so. He would always bring some nourishment such as leftover meals or a saucer of milk, left by the porch alone. He had noticed the cat when he was reading and writing as per nightly routine, if not bothered by his workload from the press, on the front porch by a wicker-rocking chair.

As if on cue, Cabal came out of the front door carrying another pumpkin into the yard with dirt-covered hands. The cat had observed him converting his backyard into a greenhouse to start his prize-winning pumpkin patch in his solitude. While placing the pumpkin on the railing, he noticed from afar the black cat sitting on the edge of the road. He smiled and started walking over past the metal-fenced gate. Cabal rubbed the corners of his whiskers by the lips, tailing down to the beard as he looked out into the neighborhood as he made his way past the grassy front yard.

The cat started to walk along the dashed crosswalk area, noting above that the light was red and the passerby signal green-lit, identifying it was the appropriate time to walk to the other side. She looked both ways and felt assured it was safe. With the savory thought of roasted filet of salmon, she made her way with haste.

However, she stopped midway when she saw Cabal look to the right side of the road and back at her quickly with a bewildered gesture and widened eyes behind his thin spectacles. He started sprinting towards her; his hands lowered like a net posed to catch a fish out of the water. Realizing what was happening on the other side, she didn't bother looking over her shoulder to see the on-coming car. There was a blinding light from the vehicle as it started honking. She closed her eyes, waiting for the impact, with indifference as the last thought ran through her mind:

So, this is how I lose No. 7.... I had a good run–

The bone-shattering sound from the car's metal frame speeding along had interrupted her train of thought. She suddenly collapsed on the road as she heard the car drive off the road. Her eyes remained closed, lamenting her loss. But the particular painful sensation hadn't washed over her like before. The cat had felt nothing but merely a sore shoulder blade and a few scraps as she felt her body tumbled across the road. In fact, she felt utterly unharmed. Opening one of her eyes, she saw nothing on the road. Not a drop of blood on her, and so she lifted herself from her side.

The cat looked both ways down the road. Whatever drove past the cat had made its escape; it was empty. She turned back and noticed the tire tracks on the street, swerving into the other lane.

Following the trail of burnt rubber, she found the twisted, mangled body of Thomas Cabal. His neck had been twisted through bone and skin into a corkscrew and snapped into an awkward, blood-curling angle. A concaved blow to the chest deepened with broken ribs from his lower abdomen, almost sinking into his stomach. Large blotches of blood had appeared on his shirt that ruptured from his wounds, quickly dying his white cotton. In the end, Cabal resembled a rag doll, ending up at a lamp post on the grassy part of the sidewalk. She stared blankly at the body and slowly approached him. He may have been ejected from his spot, the impact crushing some ribs and creating the concaving blow. In this way, she imagined that the force continued to propel him across the tarred road, like rolling over a bed of nails, tearing through the muscle, and leaving behind specks of blood to his resting place. He'd suddenly stop as he collided into the concrete slope. Judging by the damage, she had guessed it had been a big rig-truck vehicle that shot the poor man off the road with such a tremendous amount of force and speed. After all, it seemed evident that the lamppost had become misshaped as Cabal craned like a warped beam of iron as it resembled a weeping willow tree. The crash broke the glass across the ground, and the bulb splintered with an exposed light filament that sparked inconsistently.

Remembering Cabal, however, she finally walked by his side, noticing that his head wound had left partially as a compound fracture with the neck bone sticking out. It looked like an oozing fountain of dark fruit punch, but she knew better to lick a taste. Cabal's eyes rolled to the back of his head with blood rolling down his face. He was undoubtedly in an unpleasant condition, but she had seen worse in her days living out her lives.

The cat bowed her head and shook it slightly in disappointment. Why value human life over that of an ordinary-looking 'alley' cat? She had concluded her respects or otherwise business to the recently deceased and accepted her loss, at last, feeling no guilt or responsibility for Cabal initially. She was no longer going to stand there, left unfed, and so returned to her search with determination. As she turned to start her journey towards the neighborhood, leaving Cabal to the discovery and disposal of his fellow peers, it only took her a few steps when she felt a sudden sickly churning in her stomach. It wasn't hunger. It was something foreign and new to her.

She turned her head, looking back at Cabal and then back to the street. Then back to his corpse. It didn't take long for her to realize what she was feeling for the first time, having been treated by the one human mortal since the fall of the pharaonic era. When the Nile was still young, she felt such adoration from others, and while she couldn't bear the shame of admitting it, she felt a connection unspoken during these long years with Cabal in the Town. Some moments of silence had passed, the time spent contemplating her next move. With some hesitance and a sigh, she reasoned that it would be easier to have Cabal back then to spend all night in solitary preservation.

You better treat me to some swordfish for this someday, she pondered to herself.

The cat crept back to Cabal, cussing underneath her breath, and rolled up into his collapsed lap. She growled, telling herself that it was for her benefit and not paying a type of debt. With that, she curled into a ball-formation and waited for Cabal to wake up:

Soon Cabal's corpse started to move on its own, inch by inch. Bones began snapping back into position, organs being pumped back into sections, puddles of blood sweeping back into wounds as they closed together like seamless stitches. His ribs had started to meld and grow into place while fragments of skin mended together like patchwork till any scars seemed invisible. The clothes became clean, his shirt pressed, and white, and the pants mended themselves like new. Even the glasses on his nose were fixed and reformed perfectly centered on the bridge of his nose. Finally, Cabal snapped his head back on his neck, and his torso twisted around with his back against the lamp post at last. All the while, the lights from the street lamp were flickering as pieces floated back into the bulb shape, the metal post groaning as it smithed into its towering height. The ground quaked, an ominous wind filled the air as all evidence of the accident was wiped clean from the slate of the world.

Cabel's eyes sprang open. He sat there with his back leaning against the lamp post. Looking around, he found the cat between his legs, looking at him with her brilliant golden eyes. They stared at each other for some time, and she tilted her head to one side with a curious look as if she were trying to find out what he was thinking. It didn't feel natural to him, but he couldn't decide what it was. There were a few pieces of memory that were simply gone. He stared at the road, then at the cat, and then blankly into space.

"........ OH GOD!" he gasped; a delayed jolt of fright ran up his spine. Then he looked around bewildered while the cat cleaned her paws with a tongue. She was too exhausted to give him all the answers, the transaction leaving her spent. A piece of ancient magic, as well as her life, had left the world after all.

"... No, that didn't... happen," Cabal convinced himself.

He started to stroke her fur, almost absent-mindedly, for more of his reassurance than for the cat. She played coy, purring in a rhythm until she grew bored of it. Leaping from his lap, she sprinted towards his house, wanting to gain entrance to her prized redemption: a meal, a warm hearthstone, and a place to sleep in peace. Cabal felt he needed to move, not wishing to remain centered in the area any longer, so he took the cat as his excuse. He walked carefully through his lawn, attempting to retrace his steps:

"I got out from the greenhouse... brought back a pumpkin... and placed it on the railing..." he began, taking the steps up to the front door, leaning over and patting the same pumpkin for recollection. He turned around, his back to the door (to the cat's annoyance), and looked straight ahead:

"Then, I looked out... past the street... and saw you..." he gestured at her, not looking down but still waving his hands at the cat. She rolled her eyes, tossed her head, and with a low whine, tugged at his pant sleeves with a bite. She pulled and pulled back towards the door, softly growling for him to open the house to her like an impatient guest.

"Huh? .... Oh, right... sorry-" he turned briefly, unlocking the door and creaked the door open for her. She swiftly entered but left Cabal in the same daze.

"Then, I sa-saw the truck... and he wouldn't slow down... so I... MUST'VE... there's just no-no-no other way... I could've..." he stammered, walking to the house and closing the door behind him.

"Don't forget to lock the door!" the cat called out from the kitchen.

"What? .... OH, right," he turned the key and started his way back to the hallway of his empty house. Only the cat was allowed in, and there was no one else besides him. Alone...

He stopped midway, realizing the significance of that thought with an utterly dumbfounded expression in his eyes with a gaping mouth. He turned his head and stared out into the hallway, watching the doorway and hoping he was hallucinating or still in shock. The cat poked her head out, the same coy expression in her eyes:

"Meow?"

END OF THE NIGHT

October 20th

The Witch

It was an early evening the following day, and a young lady entered the vacant room with a bag over her shoulder. The girl was a high school student, by the name of Abigail, from the neighborhood initially, but she had recently left the Town during the weekend as per the arrangement allowed on the occasional week. She pulled the cord on the fan, and the room glowed a faint orange light from the old, beaten bulb. Flinging the bag off her shoulder onto the mattress, she yawned and made her way to the desk sitting by the window. She sat down on the rolling chair and spun around to see the room.

Nothing had changed. Abigail's father had left her room exactly as it was before the divorce, for which she was grateful and happy; the state of the room, not the divorce. Her preppy mother always tried to change everything around her to craft her into her mother's image. She felt that her daughter was obscenely dark for her so-called 'rebellious' age. The room was painted orange with the ceiling, window, and door painted pitch-black. A few posters of various music bands varying from rock, metal, punk, and other indie albums. Her curtains, a faded black, on the only window looking out onto the front yard, partially eaten by moths and shredded into ribbons. The desk was vintage-looking with old-fashioned maple wood carvings, with a few candles on the smooth, dark brown platform that melted onto the surface. Next to it were the small, three-shelved bookcases with various old, torn, and even rot-coated books that she would collect from places from around the world. Lastly, the closet with its old, shuttered doors that peeled white painting off as the heavy padlock, wrapped around the handles, would jingle and rub against the wood when opened with her key. However, the room at her mother's apartment was too bright and soft with its clean white wallpaper and curtainless windows for her taste. Her mother was undoubtedly vain; she didn't want to go unnoticed by her neighbors in the high-strung city. It was nice to find familiar, sober surroundings.

"God I missed this old house! Mama can be so constricting sometimes," she complained.

She hung her head against the cushioned headrest of the chair, looking up at the black ceiling, gripping the rough corners of the armrests. Running her hand through her long raven-colored hair, she sighed as boredom crept along with her toes up to her scalp. Bouncing a leg like a jack-rabbit, tapping the hardwood floors, she was expecting a call from a personal friend.

At last, her cellphone in her torn, tight denim pants began to vibrate and ring, and she pulled it out from the pocket with some difficulty but answered:

"Hello? Yeah, it's me, what took you so long? …. Yeah, I just got back from my Mama's house last night, I'm at my Papa's place now.… It's been going pretty well, he recently let in a stray cat and she's pretty cool.… What? She's been tested already and you know we're suckers for cats. Mama never liked them so she convinced Papa not to get one cause of her so-called 'allergies'.…"

As if on cue, the family's newest member appeared behind her line of vision from the door's archway. She crept behind and circled to the side of the chair, sliding into the young lady's line of sight. She meowed and clawed her way up to the chair for attention. Balancing the cellphone between her cheek and shoulder, she freed both her hands and picked the black cat up underneath her soft belly. She placed the cat on her lap and started scratching behind the ears while still talking to her friend on the phone:

"Yeah, speak of the devil, she's with me right now.… she's a short-haired black cat with gold marks around her.… I know, I would take a picture with my phone but she seems to hate that.…"

The cat growled softly in response, a look on her eyes that said, 'Don't even go there.'

"See, she's already pissed off and it's better to get on her good side …."

10

She started stroking behind the cat's chin, and she was calm and purring once again.

"Yeah, my Papa already thought of a name and it's perfect, fits her just right…. her name's Bastet … I think she's perfect for us, something about her just screams "witchy," and you know how I like to think of myself as a genuine wit- …. Yeah, I know why you called and it wasn't to have a pleasant talk between girls …."

She placed Bastet on the desk; the cat begun to lay down and sink her head between her folded arms as her tail curled around her body. The young lady placed her hand on the cellphone and continued their discussion in a hushed voice:

"Are you sure you want to do this? I don't have a problem with it but if you have secon- …. Okay, I just had to be sure…. No, I'll get it done tonight, he'll never hurt you again …. I promise, sweetie…."

The young lady knew all too well how that man could backstab any girl he could get his manipulative hands-on. She, too, was a victim of his charm and silver-forked tongue, remembering all the times he had said sweet things to her ear, and his hand glided along her legs. He would take advantage of meek, shy girls to build his reputation among the other men with his tales and notches along his champion belt. It would take too much of her conscience to sway her off the path.

"Okay, I got to go now. You should get some rest and I'll talk to you tomorrow…. Oka- okay, it's fine, I know…. Just trust me and it will all get better…. See you tomorrow, good night…."

She tossed the phone across the room, bouncing off the mattress to the wall. Already she was bracing to the closet with her brass key on her necklace, clutched between her fingertips. Hastily unlocking the old padlock, she let the lock fall on the floor and flung the doors open, searching for what she needed. Hidden away, she pulled out several unused candles, a small mound of warm, grayish clay, a small urn, a few long hammering nails, and a truffle of hair she pulled out from the dark corners of the closet. She put the candles between her closed armpits; the small urn was in one hand with the truffle of the hair organized into a small drawer with the rest of the strands. As for the clay, it was firmly in the other hand's grasp while the hammering nails were between her teeth.

She hurried towards the desk and pushed aside anything on it that would occupy any space from her work. Everything would fall on the floors with little noise as she started opening the urn and grabbing the small paintbrush from the pencil holder on the corner of the desk. Once she had it, she pushed the pencil holder off and dipped the paintbrush into the urn. With the red liquid on the bristles, she carefully started painting a large circle with ancient-looking symbols that appeared to be Haiti linguistics around the rim onto the desk. This took some of her time as she couldn't make a mistake, going at a slow pace and waiting to paint the dry. Abigail took an hour before it was done thoroughly. Once convinced it was a perfect paint

job and finally dried on the wood, she moved to the more exciting task and started modeling the clay into a hand-held figurine.

She wasn't much of an artist, but she had made a simple clay person to the best of her abilities and brushed up some facial features with one of the hammering nails by its rusted point. When she got it to an acceptable appearance, she split open the back of the clay person and pushed the truffle of hair into the inside until it was securely in place. She then moved the edges back together and wiped the surface until it was molded back together with a smooth finish like before. All that needed to transpire further was to light the candles and say a few verses in Haiti.

"What I wouldn't give to see Jack's face after this...."

#

It was the same time on the same night, but a different location with a different set of characters; a group of three friends were walking back from a house party nearby the neighborhood. The police had busted the party, and they managed to escape before anything had further happened to the trio.

One was a slender-looking boy (named Scott) with a scruffy, light blonde beard on his small chin, wearing a knitted hat, navy-blue sweatpants, and orange puffed-up jacket made of geese feathers slightly ripped and worn from use and some beat-up sneakers. He became intoxicated from a strand of marijuana that burnt a funny, purplish smoke and hid a packet in one of the ripped tears in his jacket with a clove of herbs to hide the smell.

The second (named Manuel) was short in comparison, a Latin-American boy with his black hair pulled back with a comb and wore a loose black V-neck shirt, torn jean shorts, and accompanied with dated scandals. He was also inebriated with alcohol, bragging about how we could out-drink anyone from his senior class but regretted not bringing more warm clothing against the cold breeze.

The third, final boy (named Jack) was larger and strongly built from his days spent on the lacrosse field, bearing broad shoulders and thick arms. He had curly black hair that seemed to sit fine without any comb-styling and distinctive features other than that he was considered 'handsome' or 'cute' by high-school girls. With his appearance and popularity, it was apparent to assume it went up to his inflated ego and treat anyone as "below him." He dressed in a new velvet jacket with a white T-shirt and clean navy-blue jeans, a new pair of black sneakers on his feet. Walking between his two staggering 'friends,' he was bragging about his latest encounter with a girl:

"Yeah, she whined and bitched about it but I think the message finally got to her when I left the room," he smugly continued.

"Dude…. Ha, you can be such an asshole," Scott replied with a foolish grin on his face.

"Fuck it, I couldn't really think with her sobbing so I needed some air. If she wanted to talk about it, then she needs to stop and actually say something," retorted Jack.

"Yeah… man, I can't feel my toes…." Manuela laughed as he told a few steps forward while bending over to reach his feet.

"I know, right?" he droned, not listening precisely to what Manuela was saying, "Girls know by now what to expect when a guy asks her 'out.' What the fuck was she expecting to happen, a frickening marriage proposal?"

"But, like… dude, what about your girlfriend… didn't she, walk into the two of you doing whatever, right?" asked Scott duly.

"I was going to break up anyway, she doesn't count as a girlfriend anymore, and it's not like I've been the first guy out there to do shit like that. There's not even a law against it, so I didn't do anything wrong in anyone's books.

"Yeah man, at least I don't think," exclaimed Manuela.

"Dudes… I think I can hear some whispering," blurted Scott.

"It's the wind, jackass, you've been hitting that bong too much. Let's just get back to my place; my parents aren't home so we can crash there for the night…."

"Sweet, got any vodka there?" answered Manuela.

Thus, the subject ended, and there was a brief moment of silence as Jack began contemplating the actual risks of a woman's wrath. Finding none, he merely smiled and shrugged his shoulders as he walked slower and fell behind his two bumbling idiots. Jack noticed that he was falling behind further than he imagined, so he planned to run back up to the front as a self-proclaimed leader.

He was only able to take a few steps forward before finding himself out of breath, starting to wheeze and cough with his hand around his throat. Cold sweat had begun to form around his head as he tried to find out what was wrong. It had felt like something was wrapped around his throat, closing tightly inside like he had gained some sort of allergy to something foreign. As he moved his fingers around his throat, it felt more like something had squeezed around his neck as his throat seemed to be strangely thinner. As if his throat molded involuntarily without him knowing or seeing it for himself, closing tighter and tighter.

He tried to call out to Scott and Manuela, but he couldn't feel anything come in or out. He fell to his knees and began reaching his hands out, desperately grabbing at the thin air towards the two stumbling, oblivious boys. They continued to walk further and further beyond his reach, the two trapped in their own world even to notice his absence until they were soon out of sight as well. He stumbled further to the ground, one hand on the pavement, the other reaching around his neckline. Tugging at his shirt, he tried to see if there was something he could dislodge or pull out of his throat. He could not find anything.

As the breathlessness started to burn his lungs, he felt something pierce his left leg like a shotgun shell and ripped a hole in-between his thigh and leg near the knee. It tore through his bone, flesh, and skin so quickly that it took a few moments before it registered to his mind. The pain was so massive; it was like a nail the size and length of a 2x4 hammered into his body. He couldn't scream on account that his throat was closed to the point he could barely breathe, and he was unable to move to get help anymore. The other kneecap became pierced a moment later, bits of bone and flesh exploded from the back end of his leg. Along with the painful shearing sensation doubling in power and length, he could feel blood pouring out like a waterspout that was his legs and started to feel light-headed and nauseous at the sight of the red pool forming around his lower half. He wasn't going to give up easily, though.

In a final maneuver to get help, literally with dying breath, he started to pull on the pavement surface in an attempt to crawl to get their attention; he'd figured he could throw a rock or twig at them, perhaps. He could feel some hope returning to him alongside some fleeting strength in his straining arms. From a corner of his mind, denying everything else that had happened, he felt that he could still pull out of it. At the same time, as he looked around him frantically, he couldn't find a source or person in the area that could be responsible for his impending doom. Since Scott and Manuela were both ahead of him by a couple of blocks, he was the only one on the street of the darkened sidewalk. There was no visible force or stranger in his line of sight, and he couldn't hear anything besides the wind blowing the autumn leaves. He was alone to his own devices, not even a bird to caw or a squirrel to scurry around the trees. With his mind racing to find a destination, there was no evidence to indicate what was happening.

Just as he was about to give up, he felt the sleeves of his pants tugged aggressively and started to drag backward as he clawed at the edges of the sidewalk blocks. He could feel his legs lifted off the ground against his will; his hands began to bleed while his palms were scraping across the pavement with scratches and cuts. Turning his head to one side, he looked at an angle to see who was attacking him. There was no one there.

He could plainly see as he passed by a street lamp. The darkness of the night couldn't conceal anyone's presence by then. There was nothing at the ends of his feet. He was hoisted in the air by an invisible force, gliding above the sidewalk, his hands and head pressed against the pavement. It wasn't until he was a few feet pulled back to where he had first begun that it stopped, slamming his legs and feet to the ground in a sudden motion. They were soon pinned with a heavyweight, preventing him from moving like an anchor thrown into the sea in the middle of an unforgiving storm. He wouldn't be able to abandon the ship.

In the final act, Jack could feel fingers creep along his neck. The invisible force pulled at his neck, forming as if he was wrapped in a noose by some executor. He started to rise into the air, hovering closer and closer to the streetlamp above, blinding him as he levitated in mid-air. He could feel the fingers tightening harder into a vice-like grip. The last of his breath escaped his mouth as he gurgled and stuttered violently. His eyes were burning with tears from an unrelenting sadness, knowing there was something wicked coming his way. The eyes soon ceased their crying as they began to roll to the back of the head and turned nearly death-white in his face. His lungs began to collapse and slowly die like a smoldering flame. It welled up inside him so quickly. Both the pain of suffocating and broken bones mixed into a different formula of sensation, bubbling over and spewing like a geyser over him. The feeling became an overload, tripling in effect alongside the searing pain in his engorged kneecaps blasted from the backside of his legs, no longer feeling the puddle of warm, wet blood against his skin. He was losing feeling altogether from the excruciating exercise of his nerve cells, the blood spilling onto the ground below him.

The last thing that went through Jack's mind was the faces of all the women he had been with, the lives he ruined, and how many more he would have taken with him if given a chance. Among the different faces smiling at him, he couldn't remember any of their names. He had felt robbed of some freedom. He had given up hope; he only wanted it to be finally finished, no longer taunting by this power over him.

His life had ended abruptly, and his body hit the pavement with a loud resonating crack, and then the pain had dispersed. There was only darkness as Jack's lifeless body laid across the sidewalk pavement with open arms resting on either side. It appeared as if he were embracing the ground in his sprawled slumber.

"Hey... Manny?" asked Scott.

"Wha?" spat Manuela.

"Wasn't there... like... someone else with us... before?"

#

"Abigail? Are you upstairs?"

"Yeah Papa"

"What are you doing? You're not listening to your headset too loudly again, are you?"

"No Dad, I'm just finishing up an art project for school...."

"Okay, come on down. I got dinner almost ready... have you seen Bastet?"

"Yeah Papa, she's with me. I'll bring her down to kitchen after I take a shower...."

"Okay, but make it fast...."

She turned back and looked at the lifeless clay figure dangling amidst her fingers, the head of it wedged between her thumb and forefinger. Its head was facing her, twisted around to the backside of the figurine, slightly mangled forcefully. The torso seemed relatively untouched, but otherwise, the lower half and upper half manipulated in some fashion; the neck seemed scrunched, the clay molded so thin that it may have popped off the shoulders. She looked down at the lower half, watching the nails make a metallic jingle as she wiggled the figurine back and forth. Abigail hammered two of the pins into the knees of its legs, one for each leg, and it too looked like the legs would fall off from being stretched and mangled so thinly. She shrugged her shoulders, contemplating whether or not she should've used more nails having so many leftovers:

"No sense in wasting the nails," Abigail thought to herself, "it's more fun to make each hit count anyway...."

Not bothering to pull the two nails out of the clay, she tossed the voodoo charm in the nearby wastebasket with the others. She would've been excited and anxious to find out what happened to that son-of-a-bitch, but the effect of discovery had worn off after the first dozen.

There was a time where she'd wait by the television, hoping to find a news channel broadcast displaying another "victim" of the so-called "on-going homicidal case" and see past the white canvas draped on each corpse. The luster of that excitement had lost its effect on Abigail for some time now, especially when she couldn't see their anguished faces or the full extent of her ability. However, she always wondered why there were so many deaths in the Town *before* she came to the practice. It only donned on her the number of occurrences once she took up the occult. But she needn't take any heed, she thought at last.

She stretched her arms, exhausted from the day, decided to make good on her word. Heading out of the room, she made her way to the nearby bathroom and started to undress, closing the door behind her. As the sound of the shower resonated throughout the house, Bastet's head perked up to look over her shoulder. The cat was resting on the bookshelf before, analyzing to make sure that Abigail had indeed left the room. She took a quick stretch and climbed her way onto the bed, leaping from the bookshelf to the floor and gripping on the blankets like some mountain expedition. When she centered herself wholly on the bed, she gave a long yawn and licked her paws, finding a better-suited area to sleep:

".... Yup, she'll do just fine. She has plenty of potential. What could possibly go wrong?" mewed Bastet, curling on the bedspread, taking a quick nap before dinner.

END OF THE NIGHT

October 21st

The Zombie

I do not know what time I awoke, but it was still pitch black without any sound. It wasn't a gradual ascent from slumber; it was abrupt yet vitalizing to the point that I was vigilant. As if I were asleep for a very long time, a heaviness etched into my bones. This slumber seemed unnatural to me; more so, it felt an odd occurrence to be awakened from it, asleep with a strange dream so distant that it couldn't be my own.

I was not resting on the hospital bed; perhaps I was moved; I could not see the table with the vase of flowers, the smell of anesthetics, the taste of filtered air on my lips. It was more like a firm, hard plank of wood. I was not wearing the simple patient-dressing but felt more like tattered rags. I could gently feel the ravaged cotton of a suit and the brass buttons of cufflinks across very thin, glossy fingertips as I rubbed underneath my palms beneath the ruffles of the withered shirt. My once silk tie, the one embroidered with my favorite patterning and pined with a family crest, was wrapped loosely around my tense neck. These were my favorite dress clothes; I only wear them on special occasions. Why was I dressed this way? Why are they so shoddy now?

Inch by inch, I rose my hands with a weight that seemed to be too great to bear, anchoring my movement and sapping what strength I had as if I hadn't moved in years. My hands abruptly stopped as they knocked on another plank of wood that seemed to be resting above me. For a moment, I hesitated and did nothing. Soon, I gently tapped the surface with my knuckle to be convinced. Slowly, I ran my fingers across the sides and felt the ridges of the wood, feeling the corners and edges of a box. I turned my head to the left and right side with a sharp crackle as I pressed my hands against the wood, feeling the top plank nailed to the box by the edge.

Was I in a coffin?

No, it had to be a dream. I was still asleep in the bed, and I was not awake yet. I wasn't, however, going to stay here any longer. I'd escape and break away from the nightmare, somehow. I pulled myself together and raked my nails onto the wood, at last, feeling nothing aside from the brief splinters of rotten wood ripping apart. In minutes, the wood broke away, and mounds of dry, crumbling dirt began falling onto my face like rain. I tried swatting away the earth with my hands, but there was little space, and it proved to be pointless.

I cupped my hands and started digging through the earth as it filled the contours of the box. The gaping hole above began to widen and lengthen as my strength, though weak, rose to new heights with the hope of an escape. I chose to ignore everything else until I was away from this accursed box, moving closer and closer upwards to the outside. The dry and coarse dirt began to transform to moist and muddy. My head and body felt as if a thick plaster enveloped them, but this would not stop me. My entire being felt lighter than before, as if nothing was weighing me down. I could picture myself like an earthworm on an evening, full of rain as I pulsed and contorted to the surface.

It was only a few moments later that my head and arms pierced through the grave, pushing with the palms of my hands to the ground and easily jolting out from the earth like a spring-coil. I fell onto my knees and heaved as my head sagged from the shoulders, and my fingertips dug into the wet soil, feeling the layer of mist floating across the ground. After taking in the decrepit air, I looked around to see that I was in a graveyard under a cloudy-casted dark night. Decayed stone markers covered with moss and cracks made reading difficult; I failed to see what was written on mine as it nearly crumbled from age. The naked trees with crooked branches and roots unearthed had stretched out in an embrace, grasping at the empty air as water droplets trickled down from the bark to the dirt. A small, black bird, perhaps an owl, ruffled its feathers and flew out past the steel-gated dark mausoleum close by the markers to the right from a hole in the tree.

With a quake in my shoes, I rose from my knees, braced myself as I found balance, and set out to overcome the next obstacle. I was caked with mud, shaking and brushing off the dirt from my thin, half-eaten coat. What wasn't covered in brown, the deep charcoal dyed on the fabric had faded and turned to a dusty gray while the white shirt turned yellow with holes and patches of dark-lincoln green with some mold. The suit had been ravaged by maggots, worms, and beetles and was still feasting on their mobile home and meal. These disgusting critters started falling out of the woodworks from pockets and holes in the clothes as I began to shake the coat. Few buttons had remained behind with a dull, rusted composition along with the cufflinks, my black pants were in rags, and tears faded in the same grayish color along with the dust. The leather of my shoes seemed to be the only defense against this invasive line of offense, a lasting testament to the quality of leather artistry. I rubbed the corners and backside of my neck, noticing I was missing a family ring, silver and emerald-encrusted, that I would've like to have kept on myself.

You'd think they'd leave me with that…

That was when I finally noticed my fingers clicking as they swiftly maneuvered between the strides of my hand. A thin layer of mud was dripping off them, but I could see the grim, white color of bone. It seemed so translucent to find these bones without flesh or skin yet still animate as I moved them with a chime; it reminded me of a piano, hitting the keys to make the sounds.

It wasn't as terrifying as it appeared; I was still in the constant forethought that it was all a terrible dream. My hand glided across the near-smooth surface of my bald skull as I wiped away the mud off. I would've wondered how I would be able to move, but it was too much thought as these things are often unexplained in dreams. But an idea had occurred: I probed my fingers into my empty eye-sockets, trying to find any remains of my so-called decomposed brains in spite of myself. There was nothing- how odd yet humorous, in a way- how could I see without any eyes?

This is ONE hell of a weird fever-dream… it's so vivid

My train of thought was interrupted by the sound of voices in the distance. I turned my head to the origin, moving closer to the source. I crept near a broken, hollow tree with my hands gripped upon the bark as I leaned over and leered to one side. There laid another grave marker with a forgotten old shovel resting on the back of it in a short distance. A short length further, I could make out the head of a person relaxing on the opposite side of the marker. Finally, I noticed a roaring fire; a campsite glowed with faint orange light. The crackle of the embers as they leap and scattered into the air signified there was a gathering of sorts. This could be confirmed as I leered further into the campsite and saw two campers seated on a log while the third was resting against the grave marker.

I crept closer to that nearby grave marker, crouching close to the earth, and made great efforts to not step on any twigs or branches to avoid detection. As they knelt close to the fire, I could not see clearly, the tiny flames and smoke hiding their faces.

"-so how long do we wait?" started a female, as far as I could make it out.

"Abigail said that if we followed what the book said-" shuttered a boy, I could barely hear him with his meek and quiet voice.

"How did the two of you talk me into this?" groaned another boy, a more rough and severe voice than the other.

It sounded like it was the figure resting on the grave marker, interrupting the gentleman before him. His black leather-bound arms sprung out from the sides of the stone slab and stretched in a horizontal length. This rude brat seemed to be tired and bored from the looks of things. He continued with his complaining:

"This is a waste of time, did you actually think something would happen by now?" he groaned, moving his hands to the back of his head.

"You didn't have to come along, you know…" answered the boy in the same meek-sounding voice as before.

"Oh, and how were you going to dig up the corpse?" he protested, shrugging his shoulders.

"Maybe we did something wrong, what else does it say Victor?" asked Jeanette.

"Um…we did everything by the book… we used the… um-"

"I still say it would've worked better if we used the blood of a virgin," laughed Freddy, "I mean, you're not REALLY a virgin, are you Jean? So let's use Victor's!"

"Oh shut up, Freddy," snapped Jeanette, "I am a virgin, you believe me, right Vicky?"

"Why… would you lie about that?" he replied, trying to change the subject.

"Then all that was left, reading the incantation while dancing backwards around the fire-" continued Jeanette.

"-dancing backwards around the fire like complete idiots, you forgot that part," Freddy added with snide.

"Maybe it didn't work because we ALL didn't participate in the ritual," huffed Jeanette.

"Look! I'm getting cold sitting here as it is," Freddy shouted, "I'm not going to do some mumbo-shit voodoo witchcraft and believe that all of this will raise the fucking dead!"

Witchcraft?! As if digging up graves wasn't revolting, disrespectful, and unholy enough. These kids were trespassing and committing a federal crime, don't they kno-

…

Their conversation continued onwards, but I was no longer listening as their voices faded from my consciousness. I turned away and stood there hidden from the group, my back leaning against the stone for support as the realization finally began setting in. Looking down at my hands, I started stroking the backside of the surface, porcelain-like white bone with chipped, indented remains—the feeling of an eerie coldness emitted from these fragile bones. A glacial-coldness I chose to ignore now crossed me by, along with a hope of this being any nightmare. As I scrapped my hands together, a gust of wind blew through me and whistled as my bones began to rattle together in symphony.

"What was that? Was that just me or did anyone else hear that?" stuttered Jeanette.

"I didn't hear anything…" growled Freddy.

My hands felt the cold marsh of the ground, sinking my fingers further into the earth with the grass rubbing against my wrists like clomps of straw. It was real. This wasn't a nightmare that I was going

24

to wake up, it was all real, and it was overwhelming as I tried to cry out without a tongue or vocal cords to do it. I wanted to scream, but I couldn't...

"No, I think... I think I hear it too but... what is it?" asked Victor

"It sounds like... wind chimes?" commented Jeanette.

"Oh, my god, this is so bullshit. You know what it sounds like? That all this was half-assed attempt to scare me by this loser, THAT'S WHAT IT SOUNDS LIKE!" retorted Freddy, no longer enduring the so-called farce, rising from an annoyance to a venting-anger.

Retreating from the suction of the mud, I started to slam my fists, clutching at the earth against my skull, trying to see if I could stop it all. All I felt was the cracks appearing along the side of my face as fragments of bone broke off my face, but there was nothing else. There was no pain or anything, nothing but the decaying remains that started to haunt me. All I wanted to do was wake up, but I couldn't...

I turned around, looking past my shoulder, my head filled with a warm, bubbling rage that grew stronger and hotter as I bore my eyeless sockets past the grave marker. Behind this stone plate were those devil-worshipping bastards that ripped me from any peace. They were inches away from me. They did god-knows-what, and I was paying the price, a puppet on strings, and for what, shits and giggles!?

I got up from the marsh and started walking around the tree, ripping apart the fragile fabric of my clothes and tossing my coat to the ground, the clothes that once hid my entire skeleton. It revealed a series of fungus-covered bones and an array of cobwebs and spiders nestling along my ribcage.

I'll show those sons of witches...

"Okay, I'm getting scared now. Maybe this was a bad idea..." said a quivering Jeanette.

"Trying to pull a lame prank on me WAS a bad idea, are you ACTUALLY in on this Jean?!" accused Freddy abruptly.

"Why would we prank you Freddy?" asked Jeanette.

"Because then Ick-Vic can say to everyone that Freddy Wilson pissed his pants in a graveyard! And everyone knows he's got a crush on you, little faggot that he is, and he thinks that he's competition to me!" answered Freddy, a wave of pride enveloping him now.

Jeanette looked at Victor, who was clutching the book and looking deeply into the fire. In his mind, he thought and wished she hadn't heard that or started staring at him like that. He also wished he could rip Freddy's throat with his bare hands and kill the son of a bitch. Just like the others who'd bully him constantly at their school. He had expected her to laugh with Freddy at any moment now and he was prepared to sit there and take it. As usual.

"Whatever... I think we should leave," answered Jeanette at last.

I picked the shovel up from its resting place, the metal scraping against the stone plate.

"NOW you want to leave? For what?! Some fucking noise in a fucking graveyard?! I wasted my time, digging up this grave, touching a goddamn corpse, watching you fuckers do your weird, stupid shit... and NOW you want to leave?!" screamed Freddy in disbelief.

I wouldn't wait any longer. It was a perfect time. I slowly rose from the shadows until I stood utterly upright, seeing that I was taller than Freddy, the boy's head at my stomach level. Lifting one foot on top of the grave marker, I quietly slung the shovel over my shoulder with the handle in my grip. I could see their petrified faces of Jeanette and Victor as they looked over Freddy's shoulder and saw me dripping with mud with only my bones streaking past shreds of cloth across their sight.

For a moment, I had time to see who they were:

Jeanette was an attractive, young, petite girl wearing golden locks in one long braid with clear blue eyes. Her lips were rosy amidst a pale-like complexion without any blemish and a small nose. Victor had long, slick black hair and his face color of uncooked pork, looming over Jeanette with dainty hands gripped around her arms. He wore large spectacles, highlighting his almond-shaped eyes of dark-brown pupils, on the bridge of his wide nose, with a thin upper lip but a fatter lower lip. Each of their faces was contorted in a widening gasp and eyes as they stared up at my figure. Jeanette could barely breathe as she sat there motionless, clutching at Victor's red shirt and digging her yellow-painted fingers into the fabric. Victor had made some attempt to speak but only produce rasp breaths while backing away slowly from the fiery pit, pulling Jeanette with him.

"Fred, I know- I know- I know... that you won't believe..." stammered Jeanette.

"You're DAMN RIGHT!" barked the raging Freddy.

"But... just look behind you... please!"

"Oh right, this is the part where someone comes up from behind and scares the shit out of me, right!"

"Fred, please... just... come over here... slowly..." hushed Jeanette.

"FUCK YOU ALL!" shouted Freddy.

"Freddy... Freddy! JUST LISTEN TO US!" cried Victor, his strength gathered into one sentence, his hands held up as to defend himself while coaxing Freddy to be prepare.

"I don't have to listen to a damn word you have to say to me! Especially from you: a pathetic, weak piece of shit like you "Vicky!" I'm done with this! You'll never get the jump on me, I'll always be better than a fuck-up like you so stop FUCKING TRYING YOU FAGGOT FUCKER!" shouted Freddy, the veins in his forehead pulsing with anger.

I had the shovel raised high above his head, and my arms pulled back as far as I could. My grip tightened as if I were grinding my bones into dust and gathering all the strength I had left. In a grand arch, I felt the bones snap sharply, and it told me that I should not go further than that. I wouldn't wait any longer, the last shred of mercy leaving my soul.

"...Okay, nevermind..." mumbled Victor at last.

With a furious power, I swung the shovel as if it were an axe to an oak tree and slammed the metal spade into the back of Freddy's skull as hard as I could. I heard the resonating crack and saw his body frail and fall to the ground. His body twitched and convulsed as I looked down at him and watched his wounds leak blood from the exposed gash, running down his hair and neck until it painted the grass. All this while Jeannette screamed all of the air out of her lungs, echoing into the empty graveyard.

Strange, how much power I had without any muscle in my body...

For a moment, the weight and force of the shovel threw me off balance, but I was able to regain my center of gravity, merely ignoring the sounds of Jeanette's screams as she watched in horror.

I looked up and observed them; the two were standing, a few inches away from the log, Jeanette in tears, covering her mouth with the other hand gripped tightly around Victor's arm. Victor, on the other hand, remained motionless and silent. He merely stood there without an expression on his face like some cold concrete statue, looking down at Freddy, who tried grasping at the mounds of overturned dirt, pulling himself over to the others closer and closer desperately. Freddy tried lifting his head, but he could only pull his head far enough for his eyes to look up at Victor. Freddy didn't have to say anything; he was now powerless to speak, but his eyes revealed everything. They were streaming with tears, watery and irritatingly red, as they plead for rescue. He had lost all of his brutal strength, left only enough to crawl on his hands...

Victor held the black tome in his hand, turning around with his back against us. Jeanette looked to Victor, then to Freddy, repeatedly, afraid of making the wrong choice. But she then stared at me, and she started heaving and sweating coldly amidst the bonfire. With a tender tug, Victor led her away. She was too afraid to speak out to say any last words to Freddy or me as I stepped over the grave marker and step forward closer to the crawling boy.

I hammered my bony foot onto Freddy's spine like a nail to prevent any further movement from him. A scream and gurgling were all I received from him. He could've easily pushed me aside in my current state, but I had him at a disadvantage and overpowered him. I didn't break eye contact with the remaining two as my sight instantly spellbound Jeanette. Victor turned his head briefly and moved his eyes to me, showing little to no fear in them as if it was no consequence to him. His eyes darted from me to Freddy and then back to me:

"He's still alive," he commented, without remorse and speaking with confidence.

I didn't know if he was speaking to Jeanette or me, but I looked back at Freddy, his head turned slightly to one side and one of his eyes frozen at me, further paralyzed by my form. The realization had shaken his entire being as it did mine.

I'll make sure to finish the job... then come back for the others...

I don't know if I had any strength to penetrate his skull further, but whatever power I had remaining in these decaying bones, I used on him. I swung the shovel back onto my shoulders and slammed the metal spade back into his skull repeatedly over and over again. It was all in great stride and speed, with Freddy failing to defend himself as he was open to all forms of attack. I released all my rage on him, not paying any attention to Victor or Jeanette anymore.

For those two, they took the time I spent on Freddy to recover and flee as they saw no hope of rescue for themselves and Freddy together if they stayed any longer. Victor turned his back on me, grabbing hold of Jeanette's arm as she continued to stare in transfixed guilt and horror, pulling her away and leading her out towards the gate. I heard only a few whispers between the two, not knowing or caring what they had said, all I could faintly make out was Victor whispering to Jeanette in the distance lastly:

"He can't pass the gate and leave holy ground, you'll be safe… just follow me… and stay close…."

Eventually, I felt the metal concave into the back of the cranium, and a small explosion of battered brain and nerve erupted alongside the river of blood forming around the base of his head. Freddy's body had ceased any signs of life a while ago, but I needed to release all the anger that had welled deep within my stomach, despite not having any intestines anymore. After sometime later, I felt that I had enough with his body, but it was too late to reach the others now. It didn't matter in the end; there was some doubt that I would ever see them again. Hopefully, the message was received well by those two to stay away from black magic and grave robbing.

I tossed the shovel to the side, deciding that this 'Freddy' was not worthy of his own grave, the metal spade nearly warped by the impending dents on it anyway. It made a clinking noise as it hit the flaming logs and a soft crackle emerged as a result. I walked along the body and knelt down to examine the gash within his head. The skull resembled a jigsaw puzzle tossed and scrambled with bits of hair stuck in between pieces. Half of the brain was mashed, and the upper half filled the skull like a bowl of tomato soup. It almost looked appetizing to me, but I knew better.

From a side view, a dislodged eye bulged from the blood-mixed mud, liquid leaking out from the ground in tufts of hair and skin. I had removed a part of his jaw from the collision, a spray of white teeth sprinkled along the grass. His face was unrecognizable, and his head had splattered across the ground. It was almost like I had firmly planted his head into the moist earth, pieces of his head mismatched and could never be recovered, a deep mark that the shovel had etched into a black-red spot forever. I decided to finish the errand by disposing of the body and desecrating the ritual bonfire.

Hopefully, I can get back to rest.

Hooking the palm of my hand into his neck, gripping the interior sides with my fingers, I felt the blood wash my tips with the chucks of his brutish brain squish and drip down with a tug. It felt warm against my cold bones, and the smell of blood was more pleasing than the rotting flesh and stink bugs. It reminded me that being alive with blood pulsing in the veins felt like someone as old as me. Regardless, I wasn't planning on enjoying the feeling for long. I started pulling the dead weight closer and closer to the flames until I took his belt in his slacks to toss him into the pit at last. There was a large burst of flame, causing me to shield my eyes, and a rumble shook the fire pit further with a shower of embers flying in all directions. I could feel the heat against my bare bones, watching as the fire grew higher with his decaying corpse fading from sight as he slowly burned like logs to a hearth.

And so, I waited, I didn't move from which I stood nearby the fire. The warmth radiating from it was intoxicating, and it gave me some condolence from all my anguish. In the end, the flames helped put me in a euphoric trance. Sooner or later, the fire would die, and if I should die with them, there would be some peace again. I had hoped.

Maybe it'll all just be a bad dream in the end...

END OF THE NIGHT

October 22ⁿᵈ

The Bat

It was nearly closing time for the school library. The sole librarian was at the desk, settling all of the affairs in order, categorizing the books, filing the paperwork, surveying the stacks of returned books, and more. For Mr. Sebastian, it was blissful work that eased his mind during the day as he awaited for the evening to himself. He particularly preferred the freedom that he reigned over the library as Sebastian could read all the books he wanted as he closed the building up; cookbooks were his main dish of late. The faculty enjoyed his diligent behavior in accordance with his responsibilities; he was always on time while being respectful and patient to all readers. Sebastian was elegant and organized with his work and kept everything working internally in the library more than functional with little to no error. Every day, he would always bear the students and teachers with a smile. A smile that was as warm and inviting as a fireplace during the winter.

He took a look past the entrance, seeing no students along the hallway, which generally was swarming with darting children and teenagers during the day. Looking around the library, past the shelves and tables, no one else was available to impend his departure as he stared at the clock that read 8:52 PM. Reaching into his green vest, he pulled out from a front pocket a gold pocket watch passed down throughout his family, double-checking the accuracy in time; it read 8:54 PM. He had the habit of checking and winding his watch and regular weekly maintenance to make the clockwork tell the perfect time. He would make a note to inform the janitor that the library clock was 2 minutes off on the following day. It was a quirky weakness of his mind; he wouldn't be able to function with those two minutes off the clock.

"I won't have any of the clocks perform inaccurately in my library. "To be early is to be on time, to be on time is to be late, and to be late is unforgivable," Sebastian quoted to himself.

He smoothed back his slick combed hair by the hand, his hair giving off a shine, and then matted down his goatee with a quick tip of his fingers. Afterward, he adjusted his small eyeglasses and placed the green bookmarker between the book's chapters he read to pass the time currently; Christopher Marlowe's *Doctor Faustus*, a book he enjoyed reading on any occasion over again. Taking a moment to fix his blood-red tie against the white shirt collar, adjusting his green vest by a small tug, he placed the book underneath the desk and reached for the keys to the doors in early preparation. Regardless, he would wait by the door until it was 9:00 PM precisely before closing the doors for the night. Perhaps, he thought to himself, I'll see some of the students and say some goodbyes before they leave. He got out from behind the front desk and started walking to the front entrance. Some of the shelves were stationed to the side, along with his favorite armchair beside it. He would choose another book from a frame for his next read when something caught the corner of his eye. It was a figure darting straight towards him in accelerating speed:

"WAIT! Don't close the doors yet!" the girl cried, dashing to the doors.

"Slow down, the library isn't closed until 9:00. Please don't run, Abigail," he answered softly.

He wasn't shocked to see Abigail; she'd usually come to the library at the last minute to return books which didn't bother him at all. The fact was that he respected Abigail for her dedication and friendly disposition towards him, the library, and the art of reading. His library would rarely get many readers, most of them forced to enter in response to an assigned reading project. Abigail, however, seemingly came to the building solely for the enjoyment of books, spending hours during school and outside school. For this reason, he permitted her to enter the library under the lenient of conditions, knowing she must have a good excuse for tonight in particular.

"After you catch your breath, would you like to tell me why you were running in the halls at this hour?" he questioned Abigail as she squatted down with one hand on a knee.

"UGH... I," Abigail started, presenting a tattered book with her other hand, "(huff)... wanted to return... (huff) a book... (huff) before it was... (huff) too late," she finished with a sigh.

"Oh, you really need to return books on time," taking the book from Abigail's hand and examining its condition, "-and NOT in such a terrible state like this. I'm surprised at you, you know better than to treat an old book like this one. What happened to it?"

As she took slow breaths in, at last, she stood up and stared back at him with a slightly offended yet apologetic expression in her eyes.

"I know Mr. Sebastian, I lent the book to one of my friends, Jeanette. She came back to my house tonight and I didn't realize she still had it. It's under my card so I knew that if she hadn't returned it back that it would be bad for me...."

"Alright, go on."

"But when she got to my house, she was a complete nervous wreck. She was balling her eyes out, sweaty like she'd been running for hours, and she kept looking over her shoulder like she was being chased by something...."

"Oh, is she alright?"

"I walked her home but she refused to talk about it. She also told me to keep that book away from her and that she never wanted to see it again. She wouldn't tell me what happened to the book and I didn't want to push it further," concluded Abigail.

"I understand now, it wasn't you but that doesn't serve as an excuse," he condemned her solemnly.

"Mr. Sebastian, I'm not telling you this like I'm trying to... avoid responsibility... for what happened to the book. I shouldn't have lent it to someone outside the library," she said. "I just wanted to say I'm sorry and I'm willing to pay for any of the damages she may have caused!"

Sebastian looked over the book one more time; he knew that the book was already old and worn that any damage may seem minimal beforehand in comparison. Under a careful eye, however, he noticed that something tore some pages slightly, some of the edges glossed with grass and mud stains, possibly trampled judging by the hardcover. Despite all this, he may yet save the book from the recycling bin.

"Technically, it would be Jeanette that is responsible for paying for any damages," he answered at last, "and since you're a relatively good student here, I'll just give your first warning for now, okay?"

Abigail looked up at him with disbelief in her eyes, her mouth slightly agape, "Are... are you serious? Won't you get in trouble?"

"You'd be surprised what I can get away with so there's no need to worry, it'll be taken care of so long as you promise nothing like this will happen with you again."

"Ye-yes sir, of course. Do you need anything else, you want some help closing the library?"

"No, thank you. That's nice of you to offer but I managed to get almost everything done and you should go back home now. Have a pleasant evening Abigail," he replied with a smile.

"See you tomorrow Mr. Sebastian and thank you, thank you, thank you again," she laughed, running back out to the end of the hall to reach the front gate.

He looked back at the tattered book in his hands as he heard her footsteps echo across the hall. He would make the call to an old friend in the morning, get an expert to mend the cover as well as examine any other issues that would need to be handled before he'd report the damage to management. He turned his back from the doors to briefly place the book into the return pile and mark the date on its slip by the time and date before it got too late. When he got to the front desk, he reached around and found the stamp with its red ink. Turning the dial to a fabricated date and time, he knocked the book with the seal and quickly inputted the data into his computer. And that was that. He took one more examination of the library, looking for any stragglers, and swiped over the camera screens; he found no one left in the building in the end. He turned off the lights, closed the gates, and locked up at last. Swinging the key by a loop around his finger, his coat, and a book tucked underneath his arm. He strolled through the hallway with a click of his heels. Finally, he'd get home to eat dinner as he was nearly dead from starvation.

#

He hurried along, entering his house and leaving his personal effects by the door, quickly locking up the front entrance, then sped across the staircase while loosening his tie and throwing his shoes behind him at last. Before dinner, he desperately needed a shower to clean the grime and stink he accumulated from the day. However, it was against his better judgment. He would generally patrol the house and ensure that all the locks passed inspection, certifying that there was no way in or out for maximum security like an iron-gated prison. He told himself that he could afford the chance and embrace the sweet trickle of the cold, clean water.

It didn't take him long, and soon enough, he was ready and suited for his evening dinner. With his usual garments on, he walked back down towards the hallway. He passed the kitchen and straight down to the basement for his cured meats. He had kept it fresh with a tad of seasoning of his design. As he began his descent down the stairs, he locked the heavy door behind him and switched on the lights. There was a grumble, followed by a sudden series of muffled yelps and moans as each step the librarian took made a whining creak. At last, he faced the inner workings of the basement.

From the floors to the walls to the ceiling, it was all cement. It was cold and wet, with moisture dripping like stalagmites in a cave. A metal-framed table accompanied a few metal containers by the left side with various instruments, prissily washed and wiped with some chemical agent. On his right was a long and wide container with an icy-mist coming from the corners, the freezer that contained the remnants of previous hunts. In front, the centerpiece was a large table with a draped sheet; underneath this table, an abnormally sizeable grated hole sung down to unknown depths. Sebastian constructed it in a diagonal fashion, which causes any of the moisture that slowly crawled to a liquid mass to seep from sight.

Interestingly, this table had holes that ran to the legs and out towards that hole. Above, a single chain on a simple pulley and gear swung above the specimen with a jagged hook. The basement had similar appearances from a backroom to a butcher shop.

Mr. Sebastian inspected himself, adjusting his latex gloves and apron before moving towards the table to the left side. His footsteps alerted whatever was hiding beneath the white sheet, abruptly stopping all of its movements. It waited, beneath heavily and quickly, that it made the sheet rise and fall drastically. The librarian could make out its head movement from the shape but decided to speak when he was ready and proper. He pulled an instrument from the wall; a medical saw used to break into the bone. With a shake of his head, he decided against it and moved onto the scalpel lying neatly instead. With a nod, he turned to approach the table, much to the dismay of the trapped creature.

"I apologize for the delay; I was caught up at work. I hope you didn't suffer too much in my absence," Sebastian called out, tossing the sheet to the side.

The creature was a middle-aged man, surprised; the blaring light from the ceiling fixtures had blinded him shortly. He came to his senses, staring into his captor with some contempt, only to wash away to fear as he saw the scalpel in Mr. Sebastian's fingers. This middle-aged man of undistinguishable worth laid naked on the table strapped with metal shackles to the neck, wrists, and ankles. The hostage exposed his bare hairy chest with dotted lines in red marker like a fat pig, and his mouth firmly wrapped with mounds of tape. The librarian could not stand the noise of the screaming in and out of his library.

"As you may have summarized, I'm going to kill you, and slowly I might add. I don't have any personal feelings towards this, you and your partner shouldn't have tried to break into my house last night," he said, rolling his eyes and twirling the scalpel in his fingers.

At this point, his captive began to struggle and squirm while screaming, drowned by the tape, unable to break loose of his bindings. Mr. Sebastian regretted opening up with that statement. He knew better than to say that after all these years, but he just couldn't help himself. The fear made things savor sweeter, gripping the man's heart like an iron maiden as it pierced through him. The process would make the taste all the better. But for the time being, Mr. Sebastian didn't have the patience for it. He swung the scalpel with all his weight behind, slicing into the shoulder. The captive shuttered and screamed only louder, trailing off as he feverishly looked at the librarian.

"Please. Be. Quiet," Sebastian commanded, bowing his head slightly towards his captive, practically whispering into his ear. The prisoner took his breath through the nostrils quietly and deep, attempting to avoid any further confrontation.

"Good. Now, I know this is upsetting but I'm afraid you knew the risk you were taking and what's more is that it'll get worse from here. For example, you're partner...."

Mr. Sebastian pointed the scalpel towards one of the freezers like a needle to a compass. The captive tried his best to look over his shoulder while still strapped onto the table.

"He won the coin toss, and I had him killed, mercifully and swiftly. A shot to the head, I'll be using his remains as emergency supplies, should it prove to be difficult to find others... like yourself...."

It took only a second for the captive to understand what Mr. Sebastian had meant, and the poor man didn't have the courage or strength to look back at the librarian face to face. His breathing had progressed faster in a shallow hyperventilating pace, tears streaming down his hot face, brimming with reddening skin and cold-sweat.

"Shall I tell you a secret," Mr. Sebastian whispered into the captive's ear, "I'm actually a lot older than I look. People like to guess my age and say I should be around 25-35 years...."

He lowered his head, closing in a while, reaching over to grab an overhead light, bringing it up to his face for a better look. He would turn his head, left to right, so that his captive would be forced to inspect almost every detail. It was true that Mr. Sebastian didn't leave many clues to the exact age; he didn't show any signs of shagging, wrinkles, spots, skin tags, or other indications. His hair had a shine while pulled back in his grooved style, and it had no signs such as thinning or white, grayish color. The most unnerving part of this interaction was that the captive had to stare into Mr. Sebastian's eyes. They were alluring heterochromia, where one eye was blue, and the other was green, but as he stared deeply, the captive could faintly make out a splash of brown in a section of the iris. Or rather, it was more red, swirling around these pools of color like a drop of blood.

"It may sound impossible but I'm around 102 years old, and it's all thanks to my strict diet...."

The captive could not help but cock an eyebrow in disbelief, not that he cared or believed him completely; he knew that Mr. Sebastian was insane. Regardless, it didn't seem to trigger or upset Mr. Sebastian, and he merely chuckled as he rose back to his previous position over the table. Looming over his captive, he partially blocked the overhead lighting and cast a shadow over the body menacingly. The overhead light that hung on a cable snapped back to place, swinging like a pendulum behind Mr. Sebastian. It was only then did the captive remember or realize what Mr. Sebastian would be attempting soon. He became petrified once more, staring at the scalpel and then at Mr. Sebastian, hoping he would change his mind, reveal it all to be a joke, perhaps someone would knock on the door or barge in, maybe the police would be here soon, anything to give any shred of hope. All he could do, however, was remain quiet and motionless.

"It was during one of the wars, and I was a prisoner at one of the enemy camps, held with other soldiers. We were left in a hole, dug too deep to escape and the rocks made it difficult to dig tunnels. We could only wait and pray someone would come to rescue us or hope for someone to bring food...."

Mr. Sebastian's hand hovered over the chest, the scalpel inches away from the skin. It was close enough that the captive could feel the metal tip brush against the hairs. The captive's muscles tensed and froze as the medical knife danced around in the air as it drew closer and closer towards his abdomen.

"I don't know when but eventually, they pulled one of us out hours later. They lowered trays of prepared meals, garnished it with spices, used some vegetables.... but it was always served with red meat...."

The captive's eyes locked on Mr. Sebastian's cold, empty gaze, and it was then, he made the first incision. He plunged the knife slowly into his stomach, digging into the skin and past the layer of flesh. The pain ran through the captive's body, rupturing his nerves, and started to convolute like a live wire with electricity. His eyes streamed hot tears, and he began to muffle loudly beneath the gag. Mr. Sebastian continued his story while pulling back the knife and cutting a line up to the neckline of the captive:

"We were all too hungry, the effects of starvation were setting in… and none of us wanted to die in this dug grave… we lost our minds and gave up trying to be human…."

The captive wasn't listening anymore, his screams suppressed by the gurgling of the blood erupting in his throat further; it seeped through the gag but managed to stop it from leaking out. His body, however, was slowly oozing with blood as Mr. Sebastian took his gloved hands and began opening the chest cavity, pulling back the ribs so he had a clear view of the organs. The captive had experienced a sudden change, the immeasurable pain had stopped, and a cold sensation ran over his body, still pulsing with movement:

"Until one day, there were only two of us left in the hole… the guards laughed as they dropped down a pair of kitchen knives down to us… we knew what they wanted us to do… they laughed as they watched us…."

Mr. Sebastian poked and prodded the insides of the captive, mashing some of his organs to a paste absentminded until he chose a piece, cut it off from his body, and lifted the fork to his eyes. He inspected the part, taken from his once-beating heart, contemplating on the old saying that eating the heart of your enemies would grant you their strength and courage. It was the last thing the captive saw as his sight began to grow dim and dark along with his mind:

"I managed to get out, and I killed… or rather, ate… all of them before anyone knew what had happened at the camp. Ever since that day, I haven't aged but at the same time, I haven't been able to stomach food anymore. It's funny, I never believed in the supernatural but it's an awakening experience when you become something unnatural…."

He looked down and saw the life leaves the captive's eyes, they became dull and lightless, and thus he knew there was no point in telling his tale any further. He became disappointed slightly; he couldn't resist a captive audience. It would always lift his burden, telling his story to others when he could, which wasn't often enough. He shrugged, slipping the dripping meat past his lips, savoring the raw sensation and taste as he gnawed at its fiber. It felt like he was eating a medium-rare sirloin again that each bite made him soar like a bat out of hell until it finally slithered down his throat. He would keep eating; there was much on his plate that he did not want to go to waste, and the leftovers in the freezer would not taste as sublime as fresh meat. He would pick the bones clean, which would satisfy him for a few days like a hibernating bear in the winter. The remaining bones would be crushed in his hands, having gained a period of superhuman strength, and then simmered in a vat of acid that he could dispose of in a safe location.

After years of practice, he gained the skill of deception and concealment that avoided the detection of any authorities. He could build a mountain of bones from his victims, and it had helped that he consumed most of the evidence eagerly. In those few hours, he had finished his meal and moved onward to the task of hiding the bone-ridden body, almost as if burning the calories, he had digested quickly. With a flurry of finesse, the deed was done and cleaned up. Sebastian already wiped the image of his victim from his memory as he finished up, disposing of the clothes in a hazardous containment bin. In the morning, he would burn the remains in a conjoining section of the basement, built to hide the smell from his neighbors. Once completed, he would retreat to his bedroom and sleep during the day until the following late afternoon, when he could sneak away to the school in denser clothing and apply sunscreen.

"I've learned my lesson before," he thought to himself, "I can afford any more burns... people will think I've become albino...."

END OF THE NIGHT

October 23rd

The Spider

It was a dimly lit night. The looming overcast of clouds would move through the sky silently and block the starlight. This caused the forest at the edge of Town to be nearly engulfed by darkness. Throughout the night, an eerie stillness seemed unnatural at the time. There were no sounds to be heard, birds, insects, or any movement from larger animals that creep through the fallen leaves, roots, branches, or even the tall grass. All seemed consumed by this still dark as it swallowed the once-animate green gale.

From the bushes, a young boy broke this silence as he emerged with a compact flashlight to show the way. He was a tall, lanky fellow with a heavy overcoat and boots that seemed disproportionate to his actual size. Beneath his coat was a buttoned-down shirt and old green overalls that he borrowed from his father; he didn't want his clothes to get dirty. On his head, he wore a brown-murky fedora that matched the color of the overcoat and the mud-caked boots as he walked thru a clearing. All this clothing was to protect themselves from anything that could claw, bite, or scrape against them as they made their way more profound. He had also borrowed an old brown leather knapsack that he looped around his shoulder, containing a large jar inside as it bulged nearly out of the straps.

"Timmy, are you there? Don't fall behind or I'll never be able to find you here!" he yelled, turning his head to look behind him.

"Please, don't say that, Nicky… I-I'm coming, don't leave me…."

Nicholas pushed the back of his hat away, hiding his annoyed face from view; he had wished his brother stopped calling him Nicky like he was some pet. His dark green eyes squinted as his thin brown eyebrows crumbled together from irritation. He gritted his teeth in anger, his mouth riddled with shiny-chromo braces that seemed to spark as they ran across his mouth.

"It's your own fault, if we stayed on the path, we wouldn't be so lost...." Nicholas reminded Timmy, hearing him draw closer and saw the grass part ways.

Timmy finally came out of the bushes, stumbling out as he briefly got entangled by a loose vine. He would've fallen over had it not been for his older brother catching in by the arm. It didn't help Timmy that he was practically juggling his book beneath one arm, clasping his flashlight in one hand (more prominent than he could hold), and a reasonably large branch in the other hand like it was a weapon, dripping slightly with a blackish ooze. Over his shoulders, he had his knapsack that carried mostly bug spray of various kinds. A medium-sized net was strapped and dangling like an antenna of sorts on the end of his knapsack. All this had cluttered and labored his movement further.

Besides that, he dressed in cargo shorts with only a white t-shirt, loafer shoes, and straw hat. It all seemed out of place, just as much as Nicholas seemed over-dressed for the task they were undertaking themselves. As he slowly rose, Timmy pushed the back of his hat, looking up at Nicholas with a sullen yet apologetic smile, pushing his glasses up to the bridge of his nose to see better.

"Thanks Nicky... I'm sorry... it's just... tha-that spider was huge... and I di-i-idn't know what to do," he squeaked.

Nicholas rolled his eyes but solemnly nodded as he helped his little brother up; he turned his back towards him and advanced a few steps forward to the clearing. He couldn't help but agree with him that that spider was as bulky as his hand, and that wasn't including the legs. If it had crawled any closer to Timmy, he would've done the same thing. He held a responsibility as the older brother, and he needed to keep Timmy safe. He looked past his shoulder and eyed Timmy as he began dusting himself off.

"If you didn't like spiders, you shouldn't have picked them in the first place for our project... hand me that branch, you'll drop your flashlight and book with all that weight...."

Timmy looked at the branch, not realizing he was still carrying it and began to flinch for a moment. He gladly handed the bough to Nicholas, turning his head away and closing his eyes tightly. As Nicholas reached over, he squirmed from the sight of the torn spider limps hooked on the slender, leafy branch. It dripped its ooze further, and he swore the legs were still twitching. Nicholas was glad that Timmy wasn't watching him at that moment; he couldn't appear weak or timid in front of him now.

Nevertheless, he decided to keep hold of the branch if anything else were to try to take them by surprise again. When Timmy felt Nicholas take charge of possession, at last, he frantically wiped his hands on the ends of his shorts like a towel. He was on the verge of tears from all of this stress and trauma; secretly, he couldn't bear having his brother be disappointed or angry at him.

"I-I'm sorry… it was all that was left to choose from… I… I wanted to do the praying mantis…."

"That'd be easier to find…." Nicholas agreed, looking around at more shrubs and bushes.

"At least Mr. Sebastian was nce enough to help me find a book on tem… we'll know which ones are… poisonous," he winced at the utterance but regained some composure. He felt a wave of pride and happiness, knowing he could be of some help to his brother and their search.

"Ugh, Mr. Sebastian always creeps me out…. ALWAYS. You never see him outside the library or his house. He's like some vampire or something…."

"I think he's cool… and he's nice to me…." Timmy mumbled, more to himself than to Nicholas.

Nicholas turned slightly, giving Timmy a unique expression, wondering what his brother saw in a freak like that librarian. He had hoped Timmy wouldn't grow up to be like him, roaming around the bookshelves like some automated machine. His eyes transformed into a more bewildered look as he dropped his bag and rushed back to Timmy's side once more.

"Timmy, don't move."

"Wh-wh-wh-what? Why?! Is it an-nothe-"

"You're bleeding," he barked.

Timmy glanced down and found his left leg trickling with blood, running down from his kneecap to his foot. It didn't appear deep, but the scratched mark pulled back the skin in a nasty appearance, exposing a fine layer of muscle. The blood was slowly oozing from the incision but in large quantity, and part of Nicholas had reasoned it might have been from a thorny bush or tree bark. Another aspect of him feared it was from the spider, and that only cause him to become paranoid about the possibility of an infection or worse. In any case, Timmy tensed up on the spot and looked away.

"I told you to wear pants for this EXACT reason, I knew you were going to get hurt! I shouldn't have brought you with me. Now it's getting too late," he groaned under his breath.

"I… I just wanted to help… I'm sorr-"

"Just stop apologizing, I'll get it wrapped up JUST. Stay. Still," commanded Nicholas.

Nicholas knelt down, so he was eye-leveled onto Timmy's knee. He reached into Timmy's bag, pulled out a small first-aid kid he had smuggled among the bug sprays. He opened the lid and searched for the antiseptic wipes and disinfectant ointment like he was a doctor on the operating table. When he found them in the compartments, at last, Nicholas began wiping with the antiseptic first, then drying the area quickly. He gave Timmy a cocked eyebrow as if to signal an unspoken warning that this ointment would sting him next. The little boy closed his eyes, nodding back, and it was then that Nicholas started dabbing the wound with the disinfectant. Timmy cringed once or twice, but his mouth remained closed, biting a lip as Nicholas continued the treatment. When Nicholas was satisfied with how he cleaned it up, he applied the sterile padding to the area and began wrapping with the white-gauze over the knee at last.

As Nicholas kept to his work, there were brief instances where Timmy would look down at his older brother. From what he could tell, he saw a menacing scowl over Nicholas' face, his eyes hardened and cold as he calculated each strand of gauze. It felt to Timmy that Nicholas had nothing but contempt; becoming distant towards Timmy has proven to be a hindrance, if not an annoyance, throughout this engulfing night.

The very thought made Timmy's eyeshot and watery as his eyelids began to well up with tears. He only wanted to be with his brother, and he couldn't even do that right, he thought.

"I'm sorry...."

Nicholas felt a sharp peg of guilt him like buckshot; he hadn't intended to make his brother feel this ashamed. Nicholas admitted that he found his clinginess a hassle. Still, he was madder at himself and the situation they were in currently. Nicholas always had trouble conveying his feelings to words, especially when he lost control, but that wouldn't be his excuse. He knew all too well that his little brother would never intend to cause any harm or inconvenience; he knew Timmy loved him too much for that. For that reason, however, it hurt Nicholas more than it hurt Timmy. He never tells him enough about how much he loved him since he was a baby in his arms:

"I-It's not your fault," he professed, trying to be convincingly nicer to him, "I'm not upset with you, I'm just worried... we shouldn't have waited this long and gone with Mom or Dad...."

"Yeah... but Mom was working late...."

"I know," nodded Nicholas, directing his attention at the gauze, nearly finished with the task.

"... is Dad going to come back?"

"... I don't know," Nicholas confessed.

Nicholas felt their father should've been the one to be here and help out. However, it wasn't easy for the two to understand it, even for an older child like himself. You'd think if they loved each other in the beginning, you could stay in love until the end, he thought to himself. He didn't understand why adults get married in the first place:

"It'll be okay, they'll work things out," muttered Nicholas, more to convince himself than to Timmy.

"Is it my-"

"NO! No, don't think that again," barked Nicholas, finishing the wrapping and tying a secure knot over the area. He rose and placed his hands gently over Timmy's shoulders:

"Listen, it's too late and it's too dark. How about we head back home before Mom catches us, it's not safe here anymore."

"But... the project...."

"It's okay, I'll help you write it up. Then, I don't know, I guess I'll stop at your classroom and tell your teacher what happened… I doubt she'll get angry if she knows how hard we tried, she might give you extra time," offered Nicholas, trying to create some excuse up to leave now; he could talk his way out for Timmy with the teacher, especially with the cut on him.

"O-okay," muttered Timmy, looking down at his feet. He still thought he was holding Nicky back, making this harder than it had to be.

"Let's go home, I'll play some video-games with you. You can pick the first one out," bribed Nicholas with a crooked smile.

"Oh, okay!" exclaimed Timmy, looking up at Nicky in surprise. He never let him play video games unless he begged, he thought.

They collected themselves up, and side-by-side, they started walking forward as Nicholas pulled out a compass from his pocket, pointing them northbound. Nicholas looked down to his side, Timmy seemed in better spirits, but he could tell Timmy still wasn't feeling safe completely. Nicholas gave a silent sigh, reached over, and clasped his fingers around Timmy's open palm, closing them softly. Timmy looked back up; he was taken aback but recovered quickly, smiling as he wiped some of the tears from his face.

Together, they softly applied their footsteps as they made their way down further past a slope. When they got to a leveled platform, they continued wandering in an unorganized direction. They avoided the bushes and low-hanging branches in the hopes of averting more injuries or finding a precise path leading out of the forest. The flashlights proved to be ineffective, only capable of lighting a very short distance in front of them. The two were too encumbered by the enclosed surroundings and their gear; the darkness pressed against them. As they pressed onward, they couldn't help but become bombarded by a thick, green canopy. They pushed aside more branches, only to be entrenched by bushes all around them. Their travels continued for some time until Nicholas stopped short and halted Timmy in conjunction.

In that short amount of time, they had managed to wander into an open clearing, but as Nicholas passed through, he felt a strand of silk brush against his face. He could tell it was some sort of thread by how thin and malleable against the breeze, floating in the air and now draped over his nose. It stuck there for a while. Nicholas shook his head to shake it off but had to swipe at it like a gnat instead. When he rubbed the strand off, he lifted the flashlight to see any webs near their location. He thought to himself: this may be our last chance to catch a spider and make things easier for us.

Slowly, as the light shone across each bush and branch, the clouds above departed, sharing some illumination in his search. What greeted him was an immersive mass of cobwebs in every direction and space he could see as if it were an encompassed blanket tightly wrapped in a bundle. Each branch from each tree cradled a wad of spider-web that resembled cotton balls floating in the air. He felt tense, but his brother's hand held onto him tighter as if he had woven hot iron on him, huddling closer to Nicholas. They wanted a spider for a specimen. It seemed, however, out of their league, so Nicholas made the call for them:

"We should head back, now..." he whispered, nudging Timmy towards the back, slowly retreating up the hill.

"... Okay," whispered Timmy back, no longer arguing or thinking about his school project. He simply wanted to go back home more than ever.

They hadn't taken two steps before they heard a rustling that made their hairs stand on ends, frozen in their place as they listened closely. At first, they had believed it to be the rustling wind against the fallen leaves, but more and more, they could make out tiny scurrying noises enter the area around them. Nicholas shined the flashlight on their immediate right, the sounds growing closer, and from the shadows, a spider came crawling out along the webbed floor. It wasn't a tiny arachnid, but something out from a monster movie; its body was more prominent than Timmy's knapsack with its arms stretched out like slender poles. It slowly crawled towards them, its bright-red eyes locked onto Nicholas with its fangs twitching and dripping with some unknown slime. Maybe it was saliva, poison, or blood? Whatever it was, it had Nicholas petrified, and despite not wanting to lose eye contact, he glanced at Timmy. Timmy had a feverish pale expression on him, sweating cold beads profusely as he started to cry while holding onto Nicholas for dear life silently. Nicholas nudged him further behind him, not letting go of him, and quickly looking around him, he saw more were approaching. They varied in size and color but more and more came out in monstrous sizes similar to the first, keeping a strange distance between the two as if awaiting orders. Nicholas felt a sensation below him and saw tiny spiders were running across the floor with strands of web coming out of them. All around the two brothers, the trap practically ensnared them with little to no way out.

"Timmy... take the flashlight..." commanded Timmy, handing him the compact device while trying to maintain eye contact with the army of spiders approaching them.

With one hand, Timmy took the flashlight with a shaking hand. Still, Nicholas managed to wrap his grasp over Timmy, tightly ensuring he had the grip with a reassuring presence. Without looking away, Nicholas gently placed his bag beside him. He then moved over to grab hold of one of the bug sprays, putting one in his sizeable trench-coat pocket. Each action was followed by a slow step backward as the other spiders crept closer and closer, all of them locked on the two. Finally, he reached towards the net sprouting from Timmy's bag. He held it like a weapon, preparing for a last attempt to defend themselves. Timmy's hand grew tighter and tighter, closing his eyes and planting his face in Nicholas' arm, hoping they'd vanish from sight and mind. Nicholas held his breath; they were at the foot of the hill.

"Timmy... when I say so... run as fast as you can up the hill... I'm going to stay behind... for a bit so I can act as a distraction... okay?"

Timmy looked up at Nicholas, wide-eyed and panicking, hyperventilating as he heard those words. He knew he'd be alone in the forest, but more importantly, he knew Nicholas would be alone with the spiders.

"I-I-I-I can't... yo-you-you-you'll get hu-u-u-urt..." stammered Timmy, his arms snapping around Nicholas' arm, afraid he'd let go of him.

At that moment, with the light in Timmy's hand swiping in a sudden motion, the army of spiders scurried forward as if on cue, advancing in a flurry. Nicholas lashed the net out in front of them, swinging it like a sword amateurishly, hitting one in its horrid face, causing it to hiss and retreat along with the others. They seemed to be further aggravated, hissing in chorus and snapping those wet, suckling fangs, but for now, they were more cautious.

"Timmy... I know you're scared, but there's nothing you can do... I can help you through. Just... use the flashlight, use the compass you brought, and keep the bug-spray on you... you'll be able to find the path again... or else we're both getting hurt...."

Timmy started to cry more, the tears streaming his face and shaking like a leaf, knocking off its branch and floating in the winter breeze. His forehead brushed up against Nicholas's arm, and Nicholas felt a pain in his chest, his eyes growing hot as well. He rubbed his eyes, knelt to Timmy's level, and whispered:

"Once I've gotten a few of them, I'll try to catch up with you... but you have to keep running, okay?"

"... please don't leave me alone," Timmy cried, hugging his brother like he had no one else in the world left. And at that moment, they forgot about the spiders and only saw each other, holding onto their love. Nothing else intervened, but Nicholas couldn't get the right words out that he needed to say to his little brother. They struggled to get out from his heart.

"I'll be back, don't worry... just get ready..." pleaded Nicholas, looking back at the horde as they began advancing slowly once more.

Timmy nodded, not letting go of Nicholas until the very last minute when he would call out the signal. They braced themselves, Timmy gathering the courage to position his feet up the hill. At the same time, Nicholas lowered the net to his body level, posed in an attack-fencing position.

"1... 2..."

"Wa-wai-it... Nicky..."

"What?"

"... I love you...."

"... I love you too...... 3!"

Timmy let go of Nicholas' hand, he felt like he would fall without Nicholas to hold him up, but he managed to crawl over the hill with the flashlight in his hand. Nicholas advanced, stomping his feet firmly in front of him as he began to yell and scream, waving the net like a madman. The spiders, taken by surprise, scurried backward but not without hissing and curdling their fangs further, ready to strike back soon. Timmy's light faded and faded as he made his way up the hill; he whirled around to face the bottom and flashed his light across the floor surface. Briefly, Nicholas could make out the spiders more. The spiders had fallen back a few feet than expected, and he had more room than before.

"KEEP MOVING! Don't look back!" screamed Nicholas, trying to hide his anger as well as his fear throbbing at the back of his throat.

Timmy hesitated but regained his senses, heading back to the path they had taken before while removing the compass from a pocket. He yelled behind him:

"Please, come back SOON!"

Nicholas was already thinking of his next move, pulling out the lighter from his pocket. He ran his net across the floor, scaring the smaller spiders away as they tried to overpower him. He collected swabs of the web that encircled the net more, which benefited Nicholas in the end. It resembled cotton candy, but it was more like a burning torch once he lit the fire. He lifted the torch, began to swipe, and stab the air, but he stopped short once he could see the spiders again. They had regrouped, several times larger of a force, and cut Nicholas off from escape as expected. He looked behind him, they were sealing off his exit, but from what he could see, they had no interest in climbing the hill and following his younger brother. He felt relieved but knew this could change quickly, and the courage was draining from him. He held the torch with both hands, twirling around as he saw the spiders grow closer to him. He tried to maneuver to his blind spots, but he remained stuck, and looking below, he understood why.

Those tiny spiders had managed to evade his notice, wrapping their webbing around his feet like glue to the floor. He couldn't budge; he tried lifting his foot, but it sprung back to the ground, and so he started stabbing the ground with the torch in the hopes he could burn the silk off. Then a slow rumble shook the earth, and the spider halted their march. Nicholas looked up, and straight ahead of him, the firelight revealed a dark path, some of the other spiders moving aside to make way to an entrance. Nicholas stood there motionless, and his torch braced in front of him as he started taking shallow breaths, the ground shaking more violently with each step. One giant arachnid limb emerged from the shadows, and then it showed another until more of its body basked in the moonlight. It was not, however, what Nicholas had expected.

Above the legs and thorax, the torso revealed a woman's upper body, clad in dense silk robes draped over her shoulders, arms, and chest. The naval of her stomach was left exposed like an Arabian belly dancer. Nicholas couldn't make out her face, draped with a hood, and a veil covered her mouth, but he could make out bone-white skin and rows of multiple dark-red eyes, raven-black hair slick and to her shoulders. It resembled a centaur from Nicholas' Greek mythology classes in literature. The body, however, was switched with that of a spider rather than a horse. Regardless, she towered over the whole faction like a house and loomed over Nicholas with his small, fleeting torch. It approached further, nearly a foot away from Nicholas as it looked down at him, then lowered her body, so it was an arm-length from him.

It didn't waste any time, slapping the torch from his hands. The monster's own hands were claw-like with fingers and nails like black pincers, clicking menacingly in the wind. It lowered its face towards Nicholas, who had felt defeated. No longer able to contain himself, his tears streaming his face like his brother before him. He thought he had lost all hope, resigned to be eaten by these monstrous arachnids but accomplished at his final task. He was more afraid than he ever was in his life, breathing erratically and quivering. Still, he remained on his feet despite himself.

"Were you the one that killed my kindred?" spoke the spider nonchalantly.

"Wh-what…"

She held up her other hand, inches from Nicholas' face, and present him the evidence of the crime. It was the mangled body of the spider, twisted and bloody, streaming ooze from her dagger-like fingers.

"Did you kill this newborn kindred?"

Nicholas felt his body sink to an unknown depth, a level he could not break free or climb back up. He knew what would happen if he told it the truth and that had shaken the core of his being. It would be, however, his fate instead. And he didn't know if he was ready yet. He looked up, its eyes freezing his blood as it stared down at him with a quiet fury.

"Yes... I was protecting my brother... but it's all my fault... not his..." lied Nicholas, trying to convince this creature that it.

"That, I can understand, protecting your family. I should bring the other human back, then I could feed my children," it replied, looking over Nicholas's shoulder, past the hill.

"Please..." pleaded Nicholas, not looking away from the creature, "he's... too far away now... and I'm here... I'm bigger and... stronger...."

"Hm, you are..." muttered the creature, peering back at Nicholas.

"I... I won't fight anymore, just forget about him...."

"... very well..."

The creature wrapped her claws, digging its nails into his clothes, clutching his muscles like a steel trap; he couldn't move any further from his feet to his shoulders, even if he tried his hardest. The veil to the creature's mouth ripped open, the lower half covered in black fur. The mouth stretched out with long fangs, inching closer and closer to Nicholas' neck as if to test his resolve. Nicholas, however, wasn't looking anymore. He was too afraid and simply didn't know what else to do. It wasn't long before he felt its fangs sink into his neck, but he couldn't scream. The pain was severe and intense but brief; a cold sensation raced throughout his body as it felt something enter his veins. It was like oil mixing with water, and the result left Nicholas numb and paralyzed further. Soon, he felt his grip on the world slip past him, growing weaker and weaker until it seemed like he'd be overtaken by a great slumber. It wasn't peaceful, but it wasn't agonizing as Nicholas feared it would be. He could sense that it wouldn't be much longer, but his last thoughts were Timmy. He grew worried that he might still be in danger and that he'd have to break his promise he made to him. Nicholas couldn't help but mumble in spite of himself:

"I'm sorry, Timmy...."

END OF THE NIGHT

October 24th

The Clown

On a television screen, a young gentleman stood with a forest in the background behind him. He held a microphone as he addressed the audience in his finely-pressed charcoal suit. He had glossy white-gray hair, and his wrinkled face winced while describing the scene as it unfolded:

"More and more disappearances continue to occur all over the town with the search and investigation growing larger each day. The police are baffled and currently have no leads to the newest entry on their list, the only witness being Timothy Fusilli, age eight and the youngest brother of the known victim, who could not be reached for questioning. The police issued their general warning, urging the public to stay indoors and not to leave after dark unless necessary. As a result, rumors have spread that a curfew may come into effect soon. We at News 13 wish our condolences onto the affected families… we will continue to report the incident as it develops but in other news, reports are showing that an increase in arachnid population has exterminators spooked… more on-"

"BORING!" bellowed the boy, switching the channel again. "What a waste of time, they didn't even show any blood or guts…."

Mindlessly, he flipped through the channels on the television, aimlessly trying to find something of interest. Over time, this became a habit or repetition, no longer relying on mental concentration or physical exertion. He was a creature of slothful habitat as well as indulgent gluttony, slopping in his own filth and excess.

He was an overly bulbous child, almost obese for his age, and it was a constant danger to his health. Could such a child experience a heart attack or a stroke so early in life? Regardless, he wore a t-shirt, once prestige-white and clean, now was stretched past his belly like a canvas. Stained with blotches of yellow, brown, and black from whatever he had eaten days before. His shorts were in a similar state of distress, breathable nylon with an elastic waistband that could snap at any given moment. It squeezed him like a boa constrictor as rolls of fat almost bubbled from out of the shirt. Then, it flopped a little past his shorts, running an inch away from his hips.

Over time, he would often be under a patchwork of candy wrappers and chocolate prints over his body. The boy spent all his time and saved allowances on candy, never on necessities like textbooks or clean, new clothes. Still, he may spend on games, electronics, and other distractions as a secondary priority. He laid sprawled on his back, the beanbag chair nearly bursting at the seams beneath the weight. A bowl was seated on his potbelly like an otter to a clam. All the pieces of candy overflowing to the rim of the bowl, he had unwrapped each ahead of time. He did this to avoid a choking hazard and save him the trouble later when he was finally in his comfortable spot.

Likewise, his room was a reflection of himself: if it wasn't candy wrappers, then the remaining layer was littered with week-old, crusty, perhaps even molding clothes, not limited to undergarments. The bed became squashed from over-use, the sheets ripped from the frame and the blankets unwashed for months, curtains tightly shut, shelves with forgotten toys and gadgets. Dresser-draws flung open with more dirty clothes (either stuffed or spilling out), the walls wrecked with tiny cracks, and more stains like his shirts. It was a sty fit for a pig in his slop.

He continued to look up to the flat-screen held on the wall, shoveling more globs of melting chocolate into his mouth like it was an empty elevator shaft. The chocolate dripped down his double-chins and onto his shirt that almost seemed to form a small puddle. He barely chewed the candy as it slithered down his throat, nearly blocking out the airway into his lungs. However, he had learned how to bypass the gag reflex, continuing to breathe through his nostrils instead.

"Honey," a voice cried out, almost pleading to him, "Do you know where those bags of candy went off? I can't find them in the kitchen anymore...."

The boy sighed, annoyed at this insignificant interruption. He yelled back, cramming the stolen candy rapidly: "NO MOM!"

"Okay sweetie," she replied gingerly, "If you do find them, please tell me. They're for the trick-r-treaters."

"fuck those brats…" he spat to himself, "…. shit, now where am I gonna get my candy now?"

He flung the empty bowl behind his back and across the room, hitting the wall with a clang, and resumed switching the channels. He would have to amuse himself until he grew bored, forcing himself out of the chair to coerce his mother for snacks.

"Don't touch that dial, Eric!" the television speaker rang out.

The boy stopped short, his attention caught at the sound of his name, complied to the television with curiosity.

"Are you a candy connoisseur? Do you dream of a simple life of pursuing happiness but are being prevented by obstacles?" spoked the jolly-cartoon clown as it bounced along the screen.

Eric scoffed but silently agreed. He was getting tired of relying on his mother to meet his needs. His mother had even discussed a "healthier" diet plan for his meals, to which he would not stand for it (if he could maintain the balance). He often wished he could run away if the thought of him running didn't terrify him.

"Are you seeking an escape from those responsibilities, where you can be pamper as the prince that you are within a fun-exciting new environment?"

The cartoon clown continued to leap and jump from side to side, laughing and smiling in his pinstripe coat amidst a collage of colorful lights spinning around him. It was giving Eric a headache and becoming dull at this point.

"Dude, why can't they just get on with it…" he groaned once more.

"To the point is, Eric," the clown spoke, leaning closer to the screen, "We've got a job that is fit for you and all it requires you to do is sit on your tushie and eat all the candy you can stomach… FOR FREE!"

"Wait, what?!" Eric nearly jumped off the beanbag chair in sugar-coated excitement. He fell short, his undivided attention hanging on every word, "F-R-E-E candy?!"

"That's right, F-R-E-E CANDY!"

"All I have to do is eat it, nothing else?" he mumbled to himself in disbelief.

"You guess it, nothing else but eating all day, every day until you're ready to burst," giggled the impish clown.

"Sign my *** up!" laughed Eric, his stomach jiggling in unison.

"Then come down and meet us (alone) at Peter's Big Pumpkin Circus at the edge of town... you can't miss it, it's by the old cemetery...."

"Getupgetupgetupgetup.... GONNA GET UP!"

He turned off the television with the remote as he struggled to get up on his feet, the other hand and arm braced against the beanbag as if leverage to a rusty machine. It wasn't easy, but he managed to get on his feet, maintaining balance at last but remained in constant motion. Otherwise, it wouldn't be easy when he sat back down. He swiped a gym bag from under the bed and started shoving piles of clothes without inspecting or taking inventory. Once completed, he wobbled downstairs, calling out to his mother, who was still in the kitchen:

"MOM! I'm going to Kyle's house to finish a project! I'll be staying over for the night!"

"Oh? You don't want some dinner first? I made your favorite and I thought we could eat together this ti-"

Eric had made his way through the front door, slamming the door behind him, the echo of which reverberated throughout the house. He trotted off in the direction of the cemetery in a hurry, lugging the bulky bag over his shoulder like a traveling hobo. Occasionally, he'd reach into his brimming pockets of chocolate and stuff them in his mouth. For a constant boost of energy as it would be a while before he reached his destination.

#

It had taken him a few hours to get near the cemetery despite the short distance. Each step he took was a struggle, heaving the weight like an iron ball chained to his waist. It didn't make it easier, having exhausted his fuel source of sugary cocoa, breathing heavily while profusely sweating. The sweat soaked through his clothes and retaining more water weight against him as a result. As he passed the cemetery gates, he stopped midway, wheezing and leaning against the metal fence, looking around to find a clue to this so-called circus's location. He found an array of lights on a string from afar, shining a few meters away from his location, and could faintly make out the shadowy shape resembling that of a large tent.

"After tonight..." he gasped, bending down slightly with his hands to his knees, "I'm never... walking... again... EVER!"

He inhaled deeply, rising back up and sharply turned in the direction of the circus tents. Despite his pace and condition, it didn't take him any longer to reach his destination at last. However, that didn't stop Eric from complaining any further. He came to the main gates, a tall, towering metal-grated fence that looked more like a prison than a circus. The barbed wire held it together at the top, supposedly to create an air of intimidation. He looked past the grate but couldn't see much as it seemed to be closed, and the carnies had shut all the power off for the night. He could make out the lite main entrance of the central, large tent amongst the other, smaller tents.

The nearby streetlamp flickered, and it was then Eric saw he was not alone anymore. He was startled to find a small figure hidden in the shadows with its head lowered, preventing Eric from seeing past his face. It appeared to be a dwarf-like man, but he seemed smaller than the average depiction; he was almost the size of a malformed toddler. His attire consisted of a black suit with white pinstripes running down to his black leather shoes, his head hidden further from sight by the large black fedora he wore on his head. Wearing that mobster outfit, however, made him look more like a ventriloquist dummy with the wrinkles down the corners of his mouth to his jawline. The figure briefly moved; his hands rose to his face. With a snap, a flicker of light trailed along with his fingers. He breathed deeply, raising his head to the light as he bellowed a wisp of dense smoke. If it hadn't been for the short, scruffy hairs on his jaw and neckline, he would've appeared more infant-like with his chubby, rose-cheeks, and puffy lips. His cigar danced along his lips, shifting from corner to corner as he analyzed up and down at Eric, giving an initial inspection.

"You Eric Wheeler?" he asked in a deep, rough voice like rusty nails. It didn't seem to match his overall appearance; it might've seemed more natural if he had a high-pitched baby voice instead.

"What's it to you?"

"Relax kid, the boss sent me as a lookout, he's been expecting ya…."

Cracking his knuckles, he pushed the gate open with a screech that echoed through the circus grounds. It was a laboring task, all by himself, but Eric found no impulse to offer any assistance until it was completely open at last. He held it open, leaning against the grate. He clenched his cigar with one hand, holding the vapors into his tiny lungs before heaving a cloud into the air. His other hand rose up, point towards the path leading to the central tent.

"Keep heading straight, ya can't miss it… don't touch nuthin…" he barked.

"Whatever," answered Eric, already moving past him and the gate, almost forgetting the little man altogether. He stopped, however, when the little man spoke again:

"Figured I should warn ya once… ya probably don't want to be runnin' away from home with THIS circus…."

Eric looked back with a dumbfounded expression and held that for a moment with hesitance. He quickly recovered the lapse in thought, rolling his eyes:

"It ain't smart business to scare off the customers…."

"Heh, funny," the little man chuckled, losing himself as he stared into the dying embers of his cigar, putting his hands up in defense. "It IS our business to scare folks… but hey, I tried… have fun getting whatever your fat-logged heart desires, see ya piglet…."

"HEY! I'm NOT fat, you baby-faced freak!"

But the little man was already ignoring the boy, waving his hand as if shooing a fly away. Eric didn't have the energy to fight back, or otherwise, he would've punted him like a football. Instead, the fire in his gut drove him back to the task at hand, walking back to the tent's entrance. Nothing would deter him from those elated desires. Not his mother, not his fatigue, not some walking sideshow. Nothing.

He wasn't afraid, not even when he heard the gate close back up, or the lock clicking, nor the smug-laugh as the little man disappeared in the night. He kept walking past the desolate, empty vendors; the Bloodsucking Shooting Gallery, the Hall of Broken Mirrors, the

Shrunken Head exhibit, the Play Mortician Playset, or the others in this anarchy of arcades.

He sped across the dirt path, breezing through without noticing the corpses dangling by the noose overheard. The shadows shifted around him, the low whispers and the red-glowing glares that peered at him unaware.

Soon, he was at the entrance of the tent. The curtains flowed and pulled back by some unseen force, embracing Eric into the dominion as he glided inside, the curtains closing and sealing off any light. No trace of the outside world behind him any longer.

All he could see was a wide arena in pitch black, a sole spotlight from above shining on what appeared to be a large chair. It had a broad steel frame, reinforced and woven like a basket but with large orange cushions littering the oval base. Large, monster-truck-like tires accompanied it on the bottom and a set of levers and pulleys by the side. It almost looked like it meant to carry and haul a tremendous body of mass. Regardless, this was not what Eric had expected and voiced out his concerns:

"HEY! Where's the candy?! Fucking ***holes!"

"All in good time, Mr. Wheeler," spoke a voice from behind Eric.

Eric stood perfectly still, froze in his place, and held up his sphincter. The voice snickered; footsteps followed as the figure moved beneath the cover of darkness until he towered over the boy.

In the lighting, this figure appeared to be the ringleader of the circus by the way he moved, spoke, and acted in a shifty yet grander type of showmanship. He wore a bright orange-pumpkin-colored suit adorned with thin black pinstripes, accompanied by a vest and a white-buttoned shirt and black tie. In these black-gloved hands was a brown-earthy wooden cane with a ceramic figurine on top in the shape of a black, yellow-eyed cat. As he loomed closer to Eric, the shadow beneath his face blocked the spotlight. It highlighted his features in an ominous aura.

His skin was an unearthly hue of bone-white, seemingly unnatural for a human, yet it did not seem to be makeup either. He stretched his smile so far that Eric thought it must have hurt. The corners of his mouth in a perpendicular triangle showed red gums and muscle fiber, presented by those blood-red lips. Amidst the ghastly smile, Eric could see rows of yellowed teeth as they ground against each other; they were a size that could tear into the boy's head like a shark at sea and swallow him whole. Above his pointed bird-like nose, crooked as it bent downwards towards his mouth, Eric stared into those unyielding, unblinking bloodshot eyes. They seemed to pop out of his skull with a layer of thick black eye shadow like they were sinking into a vat of oil.

This ring-leading clown gently bowed and tipped his black, orange-strapped top hat to Eric, revealing a white, gleaming bald spot with his neon-green hair slick-down at the sides:

"I apologize for the scare, Mr. Wheeler but it's our job to be frightening. It IS almost Halloween after all...."

"Right... whatever..." answered Eric, taking a step back, "So... what's the deal?"

"Simple, we're always looking for new talent, and I have reason to believe that you'd make a perfect addition to our family. That is, if you're still attached to your "first" family..." suggested the ringleader, raising back as he placed his hat back on his head.

"Hell no, I'm tired of being told what to do by my mom, all she ever does is nag me like telling me what to eat or how I should live my life...."

"So, you WON'T miss her... and you won't regret your decision later?" he asked, cocking an eyebrow.

"No... yeah, I'm good so just tell me what needs to get this done already," finalized Eric, looking straight into those crazy eyes of the ringleader.

The ringleader waited for a moment, studying the boy to see the genuine willingness to comply and accept the invitation. There was no hesitation or a flicker of regret in his eyes, which greatly pleased the clown. His smile widened further, which seemed impossible already, and he pulled out a short parchment from his coat.

"I trust you know what needs to be done next. You'll find a pen in your right pocket...."

Unquestioning, Eric reached into his pocket and found the pen. Without reading any of the writing, he signed on the dotted line, and the transaction had concluded. The ringleader folded the contract and slipped it back into his coat, then swung his arm and gestured towards the cushioned seat with an open palm.

"Would you kindly take center-stage, and we can begin," he requested, nudging Eric to proceed with a pat on the back.

Eric didn't want to waste any more time, so he trotted off and so crawled into the seat and sat on the cushions, resting his neck on a pillow as he sank into the fabric. He couldn't deny it, the chair was five times his size, yet it was exceedingly comfortable. Eric felt like he could drift off to sleep if it were for the thought of candy invading his mind.

"Alright, I'm here… get me the candy, now!" commanded Eric, his arms folded and resting on his belly like a pompous royal on a throne.

"As you wish," giggled the ringleader, clapping his hands, followed by a blinding light that flashed and incapacitated Eric.

When he opened his eye, he looked around and found nothing but mountains of candy of various sizes and varying types. There were towering lollipops of swirling rainbows, freshly-baked brownies in transparent foil, giant gumballs and jawbreakers in small trays, king-sized candy bars, and mounds upon mounds of chocolate in colorful wrappers. It was all a beautiful sight that almost moved him to tears, but now he'd have to get up and grab it from his precious seat. But before he could move, he noticed something crawling onto the seat. At first, he thought it was some sort of bug, but when he squinted, he could see it was something else entirely. It LOOKED like a piece of chocolate, moving on its own. That's when he noticed more swarm around the edges of the cushion, moving around on tips like toddlers learning to walk on their own. Eric blinked furiously, trying to wipe away the seemingly hallucinated sight. Still, it was confirmed once he peered at the ringleader, who nodded in reply:

"Just a bit of showmanship magic, wouldn't want our next star-attraction to strain himself.…"

When Eric looked back, the pieces of unwrapped candy were at his belly, approaching quickly to his neck. Simply, he shrugged and opened his mouth, awaiting the inevitable of his just desserts. One by one, in slow tangent, they dropped into his mouth and chewed his way into each one, the sweet goodness falling further into his throat and down his stomach. He closed his eyes, blissfully engaging in an almost autonomous motion, leaning back as he continued to chew his way into the candy. It wasn't until his 20th helping of the heaps of candy that he noticed the line had progressed faster and exceeded amounts. At first, he didn't mind at all, simply chewing more quickly, but more and more, it seemed to gain traction. He felt his jaw become sore, and he admitted that he needed a short break, maybe watch some television again. Eric opened his eyes and saw that the candy had nearly enveloped his entire body like a skittering blanket of bugs.

They seemed to flutter with their wrappers like wings, then quickly molting into a brown, crispy or crunchy body. It wasn't only the chocolate, but balls of gumdrops began rolling past like dung beetles. Little gummi-worms were snaking their way down his gullet, and rolls of taffy-like centipedes curling around his lips. Eric waved his arms, looking around the seat to find help, and found the ringleader grinning ear-to-ear as he loomed over.

"I did warn you, we all did," chuckled the menacing clown, "didn't your mother ever tell you: Be careful what you wish for? You can't back out now, we have it writing…."

From thin air, he pulled out a copy of the contract in question, pointing down to some fine-print and reading out loud to Eric:

"The first-party (that's us) will provide the second-party (that's you) with an endless supply of candy UNTIL he/she is unable to eat any more of the candy. The amount of candy accrued will be translated into a debt that will be served in the first-party's establishment (that's our circus)… or faced the penalty of death…."

Eric's eyes widened, mumbling as his mouth became gagged with the stuffing of candy, trying to break away and crawl out of his prison of candy. The weight, however, made it near impossible to add to his weight, the candy pushing him down further and sagging into the cushions like quicksand. He looked around for any sign of hope to escape before the ringleader continued:

"We're holding you up on your part, Mr. Wheeler. We need a new attraction to bring in more customers, and what better way than to show them the Fattest Kid in the World? They'll come and be repulsed, scared straight into eating better and properly… really, you'll be doing the community a great favor, you should be honored…."

Eric could barely breathe, more and more of the candy forced their way into his mouth, stretching it out, but by some unholy miracle, he seemed to survive the onslaught. That's when he heard his belly begin to gurgle, then he heard something pop and whizzed in the air. He looked down and could make out his belly, popping out from the army of sweets. His stomach seemed to begin to swell in size- slowly but surely- building up towards the sky.

"Get wardrobe and makeup down here, we've got five minutes before he's ready. And someone get the camera rolling, I wanted to shoot for our next commercial...."

#

Back at the house, Eric's mother had finished her dinner in crushing silence, lamenting the absence of her only son. She had cleaned the dishes and wrapped the plate, left it in the refrigerator for her son when he returns tomorrow. Hopefully, she thought, he'd come back and enjoy it later. In the end, she retired to the couch and tried to distract her mind from isolation. She turned on the television and began flipping channels until she found something of interest; most of her shows wouldn't be on until later. It was only then she saw a channel amid an advertisement:

"Come on down, and see the circus of the lifetime!" rang out the ringleader, a clown sporting a pumpkin-like theme of costuming. "We have all new attractions that are certain to boggle your minds! We have the Invisible Woman, the Three-Headed Hell-Hound, the Living Gargoyle and now...."

The clown leaned closer towards the television screen. His rows of long teeth revealed past his gums as he smiled and flourished his arm towards the next attraction with maniacal glee. What came next gave Eric's mother an upset stomach, holding her mouth as she meekly gasped at the grotesque sight. In the spotlight was a giant mound of flesh, rolls of fat, and beads of sweat trembled with hobbling feet sticking out from the base. On both sides, arms teetered with gobs of fingers out from the palms. She looked past the trembling torso and could barely make out a face, the neck bubbling from out of his shoulders, but she could see puffed-up cheeks along with a mouth that seemed caked with chocolate slime. She could see two specks of eyes streaming with tears as it tried to cry but could only spew a forming puddle of brown liquid, belching and puking its filth on its self. What kind of creature could that be? Was it fake or genuine? Why would anyone put such a thing in a miserable state?

She tried to look away, but felt compelled to look onward, horrified yet intrigued in some way...

"We present the Fattest Kid in the World, for a limited time! Come see the spectacle of unprecedented proportions as he continues to stuff his greedy face with candy! A true vice of gluttony in our modern society! And, as a special treat, you can donate a small portion and feed this little piggy as much as you want... half of the proceeds go to charity...."

She couldn't watch anymore; she switched to another channel and tried to shake the disgusting sight from his head. For some reason, it was more than she could bear, then she started to think about Eric again:

"And I was thinking of taking him to see the circus, what kind of mother would I be if I subjected to him with such morbid sights? ... it's settled, he's going to be on a diet from now on!"

END OF THE NIGHT

October 25th

The Ghost

Dr. Lance de Barra examined the surface of the mask on a desk, memorizing details as his eyes shifted up and down, his gaze rising and falling. With a fine brush, he cleaned the dust and dirt off the edges and crevices to bring back some revitalization to it. Given the mask's state, an impossible task became increasingly difficult to continue in observation as he was a tad squeamish towards gore themes.

The mask had the shape and exact likeness of a human skull ultimately. The material seemed to be convincing with its smooth porcelain, Dr. Barra gently gripped the edges with a nylon-blue glove. It stared at him with pitiless black sockets with its toothy grin gleaming under the soft lamplight. What disturbed the researcher more was the portions of the skull that had retained a thin layer of dried red pigment. A dried cloth or parchment separated that he was hesitant to confirm. It was assumed to be "cloth" for the sake of the researcher's mentality, but it looked and felt like human skin. He held in a gag that was lugging at the bottom of his throat as he couldn't fathom how skin and blood fragments remained intact for so long. Reluctantly, he dabbed a damp swab against the "cloth," and enclosed the sample into a vial for a standard analysis test. He had hoped that the lab would confirm the results, concluding it was only primitive paint.

Nervously, he swiped away the cold sweat from his brow with a naked arm and pushed the rim of his glasses with the clean, exposed end of his palm to avoid cross-contamination. The phone rang, caused the researcher to jump to his seat, his heart rate accelerated like a jack-rabbit. He signed, removing the gloves and disposing them into a red hazard bin. It seemed like the right time to briefly pause from his work for some recreational diversion to ease some stress. He glanced at the lite numbers on display, reading who it was on the other line. He sighed again, heavier than the last, knowing the discussion wouldn't end pleasantly:

"Hello dear, I was just finishing work for the night. What do yo- ... you're going to the party, head at Mr. Arlington's estate? ... No, it's not a problem... but...."

He looked down at the desk. On top of a pile of papers were the orange-black tickets to Jack's Big Pumpkin Circus. He grabbed them by the ends and peered at the opening time:

"I brought us some tickets to the circus tonight, I was going to surprise and-

.... yes, that one, I thought we could see it before or after you-

.... I know it looks "creepy," but I thought since it's Halloween that it might be fu-

.... I'm sorry, please don't be angry.... of course, I want you to be happy, that's why I was tr-

.... I understand, I'm sorry again... it won't be a problem, I'll just keep working, you have fun and stay safe... I lov-"

The repeating dial tone cut him off at the other end as she hung upon him. Tossing the tickets into the bin, he slumped into his seat and stared deeply into the mask resting on the pedestal. He recalled the speculations behind the legends revolving around this mask. Some researchers theorized that it was an instrument for ceremonial purposes in blood rituals and sacrifices to somewhat diabolic deities ranging from dominions of war, vengeance, or pacts. This history would explain the "blood" coated on the surface upon discovery in one of those burial tombs and why it was critical to collect as many samples to determine if it is blood and from whom. He shuddered at the thought, but it would make sense. That's what was so interesting to the researcher, how many were involved with this artifact.

It was unknown where the mask originated but judging by references in history. It has made its way to many corners of the world, exchanging hands with many throughout time. Recently, it was brought to scholar's attention how many previous owners based on fingerprints discovered across the mask. The reports showed most of these to be historical figures of infamous reclaim: Attila the Hun, Jack the Ripper, Adolf Hitler, Abigail Williams, Elizabeth Báthory, Saddam Hussein, and even Edgar Allan Poe was said to have possessed the mask. This particular individual was an odd addition to the collection of names, given his occupation. Still, the poet did deal with death, and some researchers humorously suggested that it may have inspired the poet to write The Red Death. In which case, however, all the owners did seem to be tied to a morbid and lethal upbringing. Now, the light of modern technology could reveal more. What was its true purpose, and why was it such a secret to the world? These were the questions that the researcher pondered, given there was little to go by confirmed information.

There was little documentation or visual content, such as vases or murals to go on, but with carbon dating, the examination came up with its date of origin. If confirmed, this mask might date back as one of the oldest artifacts globally. The mask would be a marvel given how it has preserved so perfectly for so long. It wasn't easy, but Dr. Lance managed to secure the position in the archaeological examination. It wasn't just a thrill for him to have such a powerfully influential piece of history in such marvelous condition. Nevertheless, it would afford him a more considerable income than before as a university professor and even open doors to other positions in the future. Maybe even a few grants.

But by affording "him," he meant afford "her," he thought to himself...

Everything he done would ultimately be for his wife, Jessica de Barra, with nothing left for himself other than his study and work. In the beginning, it seemed beautiful. The two of them were happy together. At some point, however, she became distant and colder, not satisfied with the arrangement. He had tried to provide what was necessary, but it didn't seem to be what she wanted. Over time, the passionate spark had died out as quickly as it came, like a flash of lighting. Soon, she hardly stayed in the house with him, let alone in the same room. She would only associate with her husband at certain social events for appearances for the sake of maintaining connections with fellow professors, financial supervisors, and employers such as the dean. It was all business concerning her relations with her husband now.

That's why he took the job-opening mainly; it meant more income to live more fruitfully and comfortably. It seemed to be the only comfort for his wife though it didn't bridge the abyss between them. He knew she only loved the money, and he wasn't an idiot to ignore the stereotypical signs. He didn't, however, have anything other than suspicions. When voiced out, he'd drown in his wife's counter-accusations of being unfaithful, followed by an onslaught of insults.

He knew it was an abusive relationship, but he didn't have the courage or power to leave her. A divorce would only give her fuel to her fire; she'd make the town see him as the antagonist. With a ruined reputation, he would relinquish his property, savings stolen, and left only with his wife's jeers. He didn't have an escape route; he didn't know what to do, so he would strive to find another way in his own time.

He focused his attention back on the mask, losing himself in trivial thought. Against better judgment and protocol, he picked the front's edges with his bare hands, careful not to damage or tamper with it. He looked over the surface with a steady grip, no longer fearful or concerned of the assumed "blood" stains. His eyes stared into that grinning masque as if ever cheerful to it all, and he had wished he could be as joyous.

As he turned it over, he noticed the smoother groove beneath the mask. Unlike the face-let, the interior was clean, almost shimmering, like crystallized glass as it reflected off the light despite its old age. The cover seemed unbreakable, having survived thus far in such pristine condition. A thought had occurred to him, and it became addictively compelling. So after inspecting the mask for any hidden incisions or spikes that could harm him, curiosity overtook him.

Departing from the chair, he moved to the nearby mirror in his office with the mask in his hands. For a moment, he stared at his reflection, contemplating the decision while holding the mask mid-level to his abdomen.

His red-ginger hair was unkempt; it tangled wildly in curls. His face was pale, the rings around his eyes were dark from rejecting sleep for so long, spending his hours on his work. The clothes he was wearing were formal, buttoned dress shirt and tie with slacks in loafers, all wrinkled and dirty, not bothering to change his outfit anew. Furthermore, he almost starved himself, growing weak and thin, even losing a few pounds from the stress. He looked down at the mask, tapping the hard edge with his uncut nails.

There shouldn't be any harm, it was only a mask, and he had completed a thorough analysis. He found no traces of microscopic bacteria or biohazardous material in earlier studies. This next action could be labeled as a scientific experiment, he rationalized to himself. He brought it up to his face, careful to position it right and easily onto his skin and brow. It fit snugly against the bridge of his nose, and once comfortable, he slowly tied it and backed his hands away from his face. The mask maintained its position, held onto his face. It looked back at his reflection, staring out from those ethereal sockets. They made his surroundings appear darker than before. A chill in the air and a gentle weight seemed to anchor his muscles in his body. From the corners of his mind, he felt groggy and started to imagine an unknown presence close by him. He dropped his hands to the wall, bracing himself as he began to lose balance, dreading his decision, and tried to remove the mask again. However, a low whisper filled his ears with a powerful urge to his soul, a command that seemed foreign. Yet, it felt like it resonating deep within himself. He almost felt undisturbed by this, granting it a familiarity as if a distant acquaintance:

"She'll never respect you... and she will never love you...."

He paused, trying to find the reaction or response to such a statement, but he found none, and his silence was admittance to the fact. The voice inside him continued:

"Go to her... and show her what wonders we can do...."

As if pulled by an invisible force, he felt persuaded by this voice and left his gaze in the mirror. He walked off into the hallway, and as he passed by a window, he ripped the large red curtains from the rings, toppling the bar that kept it up. If he were going to the party, he would be spontaneous with his costume as he quickly made some revisions while making his way past the front door. Once he was at the car, he began dressing.

#

It was later that night at Mr. Arlington's large estate. The guests danced in their costumes with a gallant elegance to their movements through the main entrance, within the ivory pillars and tiled floors. The men had grasped the waists of their female partners tenderly. The ladies spun around by the hands of their gentlemen escorts. A menagerie of masquerading socialites, laughter filled the halls of the manor. This crowd was accompanied by chanting the tales of gossip and rumor in delight. In the left wing of the estate, there were tables littered with fine silverware and silk cloths, scuffling waiters and waitresses with plates of requested food from the nearby kitchens, bustling with orders and catering at the behest of their employer. The guest fingered exquisite food that one could imagine appearing at a high-class arrangement, to which they began shoveling into themselves in their anticipating greed. On the other side, in the right-wing of the manor, the gentlemen took the opportunity to de-stress their long days in the corporate trade. They smoked cigars that filled the rooms with smog and dense clouds of tobacco. The cigars themselves were hand-wrapped from various areas of the world, illegal, and prized for their savoring flavor and well-cut quality. This space was where one could withdraw from the world and mingle with other professional men, either for business or pleasure. They expanded each other's web of influence and connections. Otherwise, in back entrances and closed rooms, concealed more pleasures left unchecked by morals and code of conduct.

Amongst the stairway, overlooking the crowd from on-high, Jessica stood by the edge of the railing with indifference. She wore a flowing pure-white silken dress with ruffles around the armlets, the collar brimming with white, swan-like feathers in a boa fashion. Her mask was in a Venetian style, laced with golden coils in a spiraling pattern that arched over the nose into a petite, gold beak. It contained more feathers spiking at the top near the brow like a tribal headpiece. In a way, she seemed more like a hawk perched on the rail than a swan. She took a moment, ensuring no one was watching her, to adjust her bra and strap it back into place.

She wanted to wait until Arlington came back from the bedroom, but he insisted she returns to the party without him to avoid any arousal from the guests. He also wanted to change into his costume before he descended back to the main hall, convincing her that it would be a surprise. Jessica had only hoped that it'd be a pleasant surprise; she was already disappointed with Arlington's previous performance. Perhaps he'd be a better dancer on the dance floor than on top of the sheets instead.

Jessica descended down the stairs gracefully, and it didn't take long to get attention from the crowd. Obviously, she could sense some hostility among the whispers, walking from the upstairs where the bedrooms were situated, but it didn't matter to her. She knew some of them were only jealous; the women wanted to be in her shoes while the men wanted to take off her shoes, among other things. As she reached the floor, she entered the crowd and greeted several giggling women but quickly dismissed them. It was made clear that she was interested in the scandalous speech. They promptly receded while scoffing to themselves quietly like crackling hens. Soon, they were replaced by an array of hands as the gentlemen offered to dance with her.

"I'm sorry, but I'm waiting on someone... he should be here an-"

Jessica was swept off her feet as she felt a hand clasp around her wrist, pulling her to the dance floor with a twirl that left her in vertigo until she readjusted to the sight. She found herself dancing. Her partner had positioned her with his arm looped around her waist. His other hand gently underneath her wrist as they began dancing along with the other guests. Looking up, she could see him more clearly, and she was taken by surprise even further. Her partner was clan in a dark-burgundy, almost in rags with streaks of red, tears, and holes as if he was wandering through muck and thorns. This guest stood out far more than she would've liked in their company, surrounded by guests that had followed the same white palette as she did. He wore thin, black leather gloves that concealed his hands and simple black shoes not distinguished to be anyone in particular. Either some bizarre taste in fashion or his actual skin condition such as tone, markings, scars, or rings. What caught her and the other guests off-guard was his mask which reviled everyone in sight, trying to distance themselves to their dismay.

The grim skull grinned at her as if a lunatic was lunging at her with a knife. There was a seemingly gore-complexion running down its cheekbones. She stared nervously at the sockets, trying to find a pair of eyes she could recognize, but she saw only darkness staring back.

The hood had wrapped over the top and corners of the face, hiding any follicles of hair from sight. Essentially, the situation forced Jessica to dance with a mysterious stranger. For a while, it filled her with a newfound feeling of dread. She couldn't remember the last time she was scared, and she wasn't even obligated to resist and leave the dance. Then she came to a radical conclusion, and the fear lifted from her like a veil, seeing the stranger in a new light. She smirked, then chuckled before addressing him at last:

"You know how to make an entrance, Mr. Arlington. You got everyone worked up, and all eyes are on us."

He didn't speak, but he did give a slow bow of his head to ease her suspicions, and so she was at peace and continued to dance with her partner further:

"Oooh, so mysterious and silent, it completes the look. I did think it was odd you insisted on this theme, it makes you stand out more but couldn't you have picked a less grotesque mask? It's too convincing... I mean, it's not bothering ME...."

He merely shrugged his shoulders to give a weak reply, and they continued their waltz amidst the music from the orchestra band. A symphony of fine-strung violins, chords, and wind instruments as they played sweetly. As the music soothingly sang throughout the halls, everything seemed to fade from Jessica's awareness, and she simply enjoyed the dance. To her delight, Mr. Arlington WAS an excellent dancer, leading her onward with a flurry of moves, twirling her in a blizzard of wonder. She felt lightheaded and laughed, thinking she would've been at some disgusting, rancid circus with her husband. She stopped, facing Mr. Arlington, who had slowed their progress as the music changed tunes. She leaned closer, placing her head against his chest as she addressed him:

"I've been thinking about your proposal, and I think I'll take you up on it. I'll talk to my husband in a few days and get the divorce together...."

He didn't speak. He merely listened on as they continued to waltz, not moving otherwise to give any suggested signal. Jessica continued, a part of her wanted to get it out of her mind at last:

"I mean, he's intelligent, hard-working... and not bad in bed I'll admit... but I married him with the expectation that he'd earn the right to be my husband. You know what I'm talking about, I'm a high-born woman that needs to be treated properly and that needs financial stability at the highest order. Besides, he gets on my nerves with his clinginess but that's expected, and I have been bad for him. If you can, get your lawyers to let him keep his junk, it's not like I needed or wanted in the first place. What do you think?"

Jessica felt his hand over her wrist and waist turn cold and iron-wrought, and she looked up, unable to find any expression in the eyes or face. As a result, she had to surmise that it was hushed anticipation and excitement from her acceptance. All the same, she felt uncomfortable and tried to wring her waist a bit loose. She lifted herself off his chest and began to take notice of her surroundings. In an attempt to calm him down, she tried to change the topic:

"God, this music got depressing, hasn't it? I know it's technically a Halloween party but they could liven things up," she squeaked, looking around at the other guest and briefly staring at the musicians.

"It's called Danse Macabre, written by Hans Holbein the Younger."

Her head spun back, and she stared at her dancing partner. That wasn't Mr. Arlington's voice. This voice was deep with overlapping noise like a reverberating echo in of itself. In the end, it sounded as if he was spewing gravel onto the floor as the voice bellowed in a low yet insidious tone.

"Who the hell are you?! Where the hell is Arlington?!" she screamed, hoping she'd get someone's attention as she still couldn't pull away from him.

"You should be more concerned about what's happening to everyone else," he spoke, his voice piercing her being once more.

Jessica didn't understand what he meant by that, feverishly looking around again to see the other occupants of the dance hall. That's when she noticed the other dancers. As they continued to spin around their pair, she could catch a glimpse at the couple approaching their left side. At first, she thought it was part of their costume, but the longer she stared, the more it became apparent to her. The opposing couple passed by; their masks were frail and loose against their skull and only partially covered their faces. She could see their skin had swiveled up like a dried husk with their face painted in blood, oozing from the pores of their skin. Their eye sockets bleed out, their mouths spewing out what appeared to be remnants of guts. Strands of their hair had either clumped off or turned gray-white, with all of their movements seemed mechanical and dull as if rusted at the hinges.

Her scream rang out across the halls but fell on deaf ears. She looked across the room with a pleading look in her eyes, huddling closer for safety to her partner by survival instinct. She found that no one would respond or react, horrified to see that all of the other guests had followed suit. One by one, she confirmed that each dancer had suffered the same fate but condemned to follow the repetitive sequence. She continued to look around her madly to find someone to save her, but even the musicians had turned into mummified actors, steadily playing their tune despite rigor-mortis. She looked out into the left and right wings of the manor. Despite the distance, she could tell what had become of the guests. Piles of bodies lumped together, all presumed dead, with an overpowering stench of rot and blood as the red streams began to pour onto the floors and enter the dance hall. She looked down and saw they were practically wadding in a pool of blood as it licked her heels and lapped over the unknown stranger's feet. Despite this development, he forced her to dance with him further. It wasn't the time to question him, she needed to get out, and she would have to use him for those means:

"OH MY GOD, how is this happening?! We need to get out, NOW!"

"We?" I'm afraid there isn't a "we" anymore," he replied, continuing the waltz against her protests.

"WHAT THE HELL ARE YOU TALKING ABOUT?!"

"But before I go, I believe I'm owed some happiness for once in my life during this whole marriage. What do you say?"

She was left speechless; there were no words to say as they stood there together, having realized who he was at last. Caught in the act, she was in the wrong, yet she didn't believe she deserved to die. However, there was no point in appealing to his senses as the bodies started to hit the floor in a wet, resounding echo. To her, he seemed committed to killing everyone in the building without hesitation. She took a few minutes to look around the room. The bodies were lifeless and contorted in a mangled mess of twisted arms, locked in a festering embrace.

She could've asked what had happened between them, how they came to this point, what they could've done to prevent this, or better still, how she could make up for what she had done. But there was only one question going through her vacant mind:

"How are you doing this?"

"Do you really want to know? Here, come closer and I'll tell you…."

"Wh- wait I'm sor-"

She was interrupted as he leaned in, the mask parted from the mandible-jawbone, and he kissed her deeply through the exposed opening. In that instance, she could feel a brief warmth in her skin, tender and sweet amidst it all. It didn't feel like death at all, and she had thought it was all just some delusion. Then she felt something slither insider her, and her heart began to quicken like a drum.

His hands were wrapped around her arms, locking them in a place like a straitjacket. He confined her to the spot, unable to move or escape from his grasp. Nevertheless, she struggled as she attempted to fend her life, her cries muffled as he forcibly pressed himself in the kiss. Rapidly, she started to feel cold as if running water was being splashed down on her spine, causing her to shake and tense her muscles. Despite this sudden chill, she also felt a growing warmth in her skin that began to accelerate into a rapid fiery sensation; the pain was the same as blistered by a burning flame. At the same time, she could feel a sharp, piercing pain erupt as if he repeatedly stabbed a dagger into her heart, stomach, and kidneys. Each pore began to scream, and soon, she felt her body start to crackle and shrink as she felt her blood drain out. She could feel the life inside herself begin to dwindle, growing weaker and weaker as she continued to combat her aggressor. Her mind became feral, the pain overtaking her senses as she convulsed and throbbed uncontrollably.

In his hands, he could feel her bones become brittle and dry, breaking between his fingers, her blood washing over his knuckles as it poured down to the floor. He opened his eyes and stared down at her dull, white eyes as they slowly started to recede into her skull. Her lips were drying up, crumbling almost into dust, but he continued to press onward, maintaining his kiss. The lips sank into themselves, revealing rows of teeth as blood spewed from the corners of her gritted mouth. Her skin was painted red, but he could see the skin tone turning stone-gray, tightly forming around what was left of her body like a wrought sheet. Likewise, her nose and ears crumbled away and sank into her head to complete her mummification. Her hair became excessively dry, frizzling like wires and turning white as she continued to age with bits of clumps falling onto the floor. More and more, he could feel the last flame of life in her smoldered out in a whimper, and a part of him reveled in the power he had over her.

The pain subsided, and overtaken by a slumber, a deathly sickness, and nausea that made her limp and dizzy, and he could sense the end had come. He let her body go, falling backward and curling into a ball as if she were huddling for warmth. She couldn't feel anything, the ordeal had left her numb, and the last thought that entered her mind was how sweet the music felt to her ears. Then her last breath ebbed from her withered mouth, joining the others bathed in their collective sanguine. She became limp, and dangled in his arms like a rag-doll.

With a glide of his thumb, he wiped the residue left on his lips. Dr. Lance stared down at the remains of his deceased wife. This feeling, he thought to himself, was the indifference she must've felt for him. It felt like an emotionless and distant reaction, letting his grip go and watching her fall to the ground, but it seemed appropriate, which concerned him greatly.

"We don't have time to mourn," spoke the voice, "we have much more work to do... the world must be cleansed... go now...."

He nodded; he didn't wish to remain there any longer. He knew it'd be a matter of time before this scene was discovered and so made his retreat to the back entrance. As he passed through the doors, the old grandfather struck the eleventh hour, each chime echoing throughout the dead halls of the abandoned mausoleum. Leaving only the rotting corpses for the approaching morning and nevermore to rise from the rivers of blood again.

END OF THE NIGHT

October 26th

The Wolf

"So, did you hear about Jessica?" asked Freddy, refilling the mug.

"Lance's wife? No, why…" asked Finn, only partially interested as a courtesy, more interested in getting the next beer.

"She was found at Arlington's palace the other night…."

"You mean… the Arlington Bloodbath?"

"Yeah, one of those sniveled-up bodies in a pool of blood. She was nearly unrecognizable but poor Lance was there to verify…" continued Freddy, shaking his head with pity, tapping off the glass with coal foam. He turned his back away from Finn, who was already sipping the glass and sucking off the form. Freddy began drying off his meaty, hairy knuckles with a cloth behind the bar near a sink. He started wiping the frigid moisture from other glasses as Finn continued the idea chit-chat:

"So, hear any other tasty gossip?"

Freddy looked up from the sink, staring at Finn from a reflection on a large mirror above. Freddy cocked up a thick eyebrow as his fuzzy black mustache twitched to the sides, his mouth opened in a discouraging frown as he spoke:

"Sweetie, I'm being serious."

"So am I, this isn't the first time something like THAT has happened in our little town…."

"I love your take-no-prisoner attitude, but you should feel some sympathy or compassion."

"Yeah, I feel "compassionate" about leaving this town, don't know why I haven't already…."

He took another prolonged intake of his beer, bits of foam attaching to his pristine, clean-shaven mouth. He swiped it off with his sleeve, slightly smudging the foundation around his face. He didn't seem to care; he looked at the mirror, past Freddy's shoulders. He had spent all afternoon dressing up nicely in ironed shirts, pressed pants, ritzy cologne, shined shoes, and gelled, combed, dirty blonde hair. His face, through shaven and tweezed stray hairs off, was still rough and weighed down in his slightly drunken stupor. His head was slumped between his hanging shoulder blades as he jostled the half-empty glass in his hand.

He had tried so hard to look his best, dolling up with highlighted features, applying some mascara, and shadowing onto his eyes to make them "pop" out more. He used some fruity-flavored lip balm and minty-fresh spritz amidst the fine-brushed pearly-white teeth. Yet, somehow, this went unnoticed as he was the only man in the Brickhouse Bar except for Freddy by the counter.

"Don't deny it, you'd miss me," teased Freddy with a sly grin.

Finn shrugged his shoulders, dropping back to the counter again. He continued to consume his less-than-frothy beverage in a series of baby sips. Freddy simply chuckled and continued his work.

"If you need someone to tell you you're beautiful than I'll say it, you're drop-dead gorgeous."

"Thanks, it does help... a little," he smirked, looking up at Freddy with his hazy eyes. His head abruptly snapped, looking behind his shoulder, heavily breathing through his nostrils. His face was more alert, concerned even, as he stared back at the door as if aware of who was approaching behind it.

"Shit... that's all I need now, what does HE want?" Finn mumbled to himself.

"What was that?" asked Freddy, slightly overhearing the whisper.

Finn turned back, shaking his head, trying to dispel what Freddy may have heard, and waited for the door to open as he swirled his beer in the glass. In those few minutes, the thundering footsteps came through, and the door burst open, the hinges swinging with a great force that nearly shook the building as it smacked against the wall. At the entrance, a figure shot across towards the bar counter, almost in a blur, stopping shortly to where Finn was sitting on the stool. At this point, Freddy and Finn could make the figure more clearly in-person.

He seemed stout yet bulky, wearing a black hoodie that stretched thin around his fatty muscles. Neither Freddy nor Finn could see past his hood, his face hidden beneath the looming shadow. He looked up at Finn sitting on the stool. Freddy stared slightly down at him and could see a small scar across his lips despite the harsh four-o-clock shadow around his lower jaw. Finn's suspicions were thus confirmed, answering the figure with a down-played exhaust:

"Could you at LEAST let me finish my drink?"

"We need to talk-"

"I mean, I'm almost done, you can see from my glass that I only need a few mor-"

"Now!"

Finn rolled his eyes and got off from the stool, almost abandoning his mug by the corner but then deciding against it, and took the last, quick swig of his drink at last. As he started to leave with the hooded figure, a confused but defensive Freddy came to the rescue:

"Hold on, asshole, he doesn't have to do anything with you if he doe-"

"It's fine Fred, just stay inside and DON'T call the police this time."

The two left the bar, Finn exiting out first with the hooded figure following closely behind him. As they slammed the door shut, Freddy was left alone with the pondering thought of what was happening coupled with the twitching impulse to do something about it. He glanced at the shotgun nestled beneath the bar counter, thinking what to do carefully. Finn had asked not to call the police... and it would be within his rights since it's his property...

#

Outside, the two conveyed in the vacant parking lot. Finn stood there with his back turned away from the hooded figure behind him. It wasn't long before Finn could make out more assailants huddled in the shadow. Slowly, they emerged from the nearby bushes and slender trees and onto the pavement. These additional four were also wearing hooded jackets of varying color, quality of the fabric, and length, caked in mud and leaves. In each of their hands, they had a weapon of some type; one had a baseball bat while another had a long, serrated machete.

Soon, they encircled Finn and closed off any apparent escape as they lured him down to the pick-up truck. Finn looked around at his silent posse. He took a whiff in the air and picked up the scent again that he was looking for:

"You can come out too, Rick. I know you arranged "this," so spare the dramatic entrance... get out of the car...."

Finn stood there, folding his arms, and tapped his foot with transparent impatience, staring at the hooded figures that encircled around him like an entrapment. The five hooded figures glanced at each other, grumbling and whispering under their breath; the short one merely shrugged his shoulders. They couldn't figure out how he knew except for one.

The headlights from the truck flashed on brilliantly, momentarily blinding the group except for Finn. His back remained unturned and did not flinch from his spot. The door creaked open, and a set of quiet footsteps echoed across the parking lot into the neighborhood. Finn simply waited until the sixth and final hooded figure came into Finn's line of sight. This figure stood before Finn ominously like a foreboding executor with his shotgun in hand. The two stared at each other for some time, unrelenting and constant, neither willing to concede to defeat their opponent.

"Is that a shotgun in your hands or are you happy to see me again, Ricky?" mocked Finn with a smug smirk on his lips.

The figure tore off the hood, his hand still holding the shotgun. The light shined on his face, revealing it completely bare to Finn: a raggedy yet thin, pasty complexion, emphasizing the high cheekbones. The shape of his head was also long and narrow with an aura of grimness to his sullen eyes. His bright blue and green eyes stared drearily at Finn, who always felt they were a beautiful set of eyes before his image of him turned to ruin by that rude occurrence. Finn's glance slowly descended and briefly took notice of one of his worse physical qualities. Between his thin lips, the surface was seemingly charred, dry, and brittle cracked skin. The gruff-shaggy bush of hair across the chin almost made Finn feel like he was looking at a billy-goat or a drugged-hippie. Rick shifted his jaw, his breath fuming with cheap-store whiskey:

"You know why we're here?"

"Not for the drink specials, you came to tell me how prettier I am than your wife?" questioned Finn sarcastically.

Rick's face contorted into a grim scowl, the others behind him grumbled among each other; some were even snickering under their breath. Rick turned his head and glared at his men. A hush fell onto the crowd, afraid to trigger him any further and unleash his rage upon themselves. He turned his attention at Finn again, untwisting his face to its original, dull state:

"There must be something wrong with you if you think this is the best time to be joking… doesn't matter through. Here's the deal: you tell my wife that all of those rumors were fake, make a public apology, and leave town by tomorrow night…."

"Or you and the dickless wonders will "rough" me up?"

"No, we'll kill you."

"Woah," called one of the hooded figures, holding his hands up defensively, "I didn't agree to kill any–"

"SHUT THE FUCK UP, CHARLIE! You agreed to be a part of this, NO BACKING OUT NOW!"

He flashed the shotgun, toggling, and briefly pointed at Charlie, who fell silent and backed away swiftly. The others had also remained silent, looking aside in a mixture of shame and fear. They knew then and there that if they were to survive the night, they'd have to sacrifice a lamb for the slaughter.

"Listen," he continued, directing his attention to Finn and lowering his gun slightly. "I DON'T want to kill you, I don't want to go through the trouble… just do what I say, and it'll all be over."

"Heh, that's what you said last time…" Finn chuckled underneath his breath, rolling his eyes and staring off blankly to the side as he contemplated to himself.

He was so tired of running away with his tail behind his legs, being careful not to arouse the herd of people in the next town he'd settle in. He just couldn't help being himself, a creature of unadulterated habit. It was like how a beast merely ate, mate, and slept to him and nothing more. He shook his head: No, he wasn't leaving; he was too drunk to care about the consequences anymore…

As he turned and looked back at Rick, he found the barrel of the gun directly in his face.

"Do you really want that to be your final decision?" asked Rick coldly, without any hesitation in his eyes or voice, not even a tremor in his hand. But neither did Finn, and he remained deadlock in place, his eyes were soulless yet fierce as if he had no remorse left inside him:

"I know you're prepared to kill me, and I know you think this will all work out for you in the end. Any normal human being would be terrified and agree to your demands-"

"So you'll-"

"Don't fucking interrupt me," growled Finn, his hands crackled and his fingers twitching before continuing. "I am NOT normal, more than you think, and once you know the difference between us... well, you wouldn't believe me if I told you."

"Oh give me a fucking break," he spat.

"Then do it...." Finn grabbed the gun barrel, held it steady between his eyes, and waited for Rick. The two didn't move a muscle, and Rick found himself looking at Finn with a dumbfounded expression, not understanding what was happening. He began to squeeze the trigger, expecting Finn to notice and break his composure. Still, Finn kept standing tall, not quivering in defeat or begging for his life. Rick wasn't going to back down, but he couldn't figure what Finn's plan was.

"... goddamnit*"

He pulled the trigger and released his load onto Finn's face, splattering the remains onto the pavement and nearby cars. The body flung to the ground, hitting the truck behind Finn with a loud crack and resounding, metallic thud throughout the parking lot. As the headless body smacked against the entrails of the brain, practically a smear against the hood of the car, the others fell backward and started to scramble back to their feet. They could hardly control themselves, fighting the urge to puke, but they all had planned to leave little behind for law enforcement. This plan didn't stop some of them from sobbing to themselves. The remaining bunch began to hyperventilate and run their hands across their heads and faces.

"FUCK! YOU ACTUALLY DID IT YOU FUC-"

"Shut. The hell. Up." Rick commanded, still holding the gun in the air. He looked down at the body, then placed the barrel on his shoulder.

"We're leaving the body behind here, Fred will be out soon so we can't get rid of Finn now...."

He kept looking down at Finn, still remembering his face before he blew it up. He could recall each detail so vividly, including the parts that exploded off of him. In his mind, the scene seemed to play in slow motion and could paint a picture of the exact moment when his upper face began to splitter into pieces, almost like a jigsaw puzzle.

He turned around, facing his accomplices and surveying the area, taking note of whether any parts of Finn had touched his face and clothes. In that brief time, he counted each one, categorized each of their names, memorized their faces and addresses, and assessed the risk they posed to him. Luckily, they had all followed their orders, wearing the clothes and disposable gloves, among other things such as their concealed faces. He was ready to move:

"Let's move, we've got a few minutes before the police show up. We have to reach the lake, and dispose the weapons and clothes there. After that, we can make alibis for each other so recite your stories on the way bac-"

Rick thought it was his imagination, the wind blowing twigs and branches together in the winter night-breeze, but he saw the others look at each other. They all could hear the sound of something snapping and shattering like bone in rapid successions, coming from behind him.

Then it stopped without warning.

Charlie was the first to turn and look and the first to answer:

"... uh, Rick... where's the body?"

Rick turned, thinking Charlie was trying to be funny or intimidate him, but as he stared down at the pavement, expecting to see the body lay there, he didn't even see any blood on the road left behind by Finn. Charlie turned back, facing Rick with a bewildered look on his face, hoping he'd have an answer. He would find one quickly but not from Rick as the lights from the lamppost flickered for a brief second. Briefly, it hid Charlie and the others in the shadows, only able to hear something run across the thicket. Then an unseen force pulled Charlie, carrying him before the lights could come back on in full view. Charlie left the group without a sound, and the group saw only a blur before they heard the muffled scream that was cut away by the sound of something tearing into the flesh.

It was instant.

"What the fuck is happening Rick! WHAT THE HELL HAPPENED TO CHARLIE!"

"SHUT UP, calm down and huddle together! Close the gap!"

At his call, they followed his example and began to circle to rid themselves of any blind spots. They found themselves wheeling in all directions, trying to peer through the surrounding forestry and darkness. They tried to look past the cars and into houses, tracking any footsteps in the snow, looking for any sign of movement. There was only the sound of the rustling leaves and the occasional caw of the crow flying above them. In that deathly silence, they started to reel their minds at the possibilities, imagining what was lurking behind the scenes. But nothing they could rationalize seemed to fit the situation. They could only point their weapons aimlessly in the air, hoping they find something in their line of sight before they were taken off-guard. They continued their search, taking turns and erratically swiping their eyesight as they could.

Then they heard a low growl, not like a dog but something more feral and beastly. It had an air of calm as if you could feel the coming lightning strike from a storm. They dropped their heads low, squaring their shoulders and the hands twisted harshly on the handles of their offensive objects.

"Maybe it's… Finn… he's trying to scare us?" said Greg, the shorter hooded figure, trying to maintain his hold on the weapon.

"Yeah… but… why is making those sounds…" said Steven, the portly hooded figure,

"Shut up, listen…" whispered Mort, the third and last member, trying to discern the source.

All Rick knew was that he killed Finn. It wasn't a joke or a trick. He had him cornered; he pulled the shotgun and fired a live round; it tore through the skull like a firecracker in a melon. There was something out there that he didn't plan on meeting tonight, and there was only one idea that ran through his imagination.

"It's just an animal, probably scavenging off Finn's corpse… we can take it on ourselves, just get ready…" reassured Rick, reloading the shells into the shotgun from his pockets.

That was when Greg and Steven were the next victims but not before being the first to see their captor in the light at last. Something had covered their mouths completely, but they would've been speechless otherwise, their eyes telling the story better than words. Rick and his previous companion, Mort had turned to face whatever was attacking them. Still, they weren't ready to face the horrible truth. It couldn't be the truth; it seemed like a dark fairytale come to life.

The two were held up to the creature's eyes, towering over the group by several feet like a massive bear but pulsing with lean, toned muscle. Its claws had utterly wrapped around their faces with only their petrified, widen eyes undeterred from view. Their eyes were bulging out as the creature tighten its grip, the two struggling and kicking, forced to look at the beast further as they began to lose air. Its mouth opened to reveal its gigantic canine teeth, looking at the two hungrily with its dark-yellowed eyes, but it knew there'd be time for that later. Its body seemed humanoid but covered with black fur, its hind legs stood erect, and its head resembled a wolf.

With a snap of its thumb against their heads, he broke their necks and separated their spine, which dislocated their heads, lagging in a crooked manner as if a hangman noose hung them. The creature flung the bodies at the remaining two living attackers with a gust of mighty force, knocking them down to the ground. They struggled to get up. Rick was the first while Mort kept kicking and whimpering, but it wasn't long before the creature was on top of him and the pile, crouched down to the ground. The beast raised its claws over the dogpile and began stabbing through the corpse. It went cleanly into Mort, tearing through the flesh as quickly as scissors to paper. His cries were muffled by the body smothering him, and he could only gurgle out pleas as the beast continued its frenzied onslaught without mercy.

Rick got to his feet, his hands trembling and the handle of the shotgun loose, but he tried to aim the muzzle at the beast. It stopped, releasing his claws from out of the bodies, both spewing blood and entails onto the black pavement. The beast licked its claws and then looked up at Rick, wild-eyed and grinding its bloodied teeth. It licked its mouth and rose back up to its towering height. Rick had to adjust his shotgun up high as if he were looking up at the sky. He couldn't control himself and fire again prematurely. Still, the beast anticipated the shot, swiftly moving to the side like lighting and dodging the buckshot entirely with ease. The beast grinned, leaping towards Rick, smacking him against the hard stone pavement.

The beast had crushed his legs with its enormous pawed feet. One hand was wrapped around Rick's chest and pinned firmly against the surface, and he was unable to move from the spot. The other hand had its claws shoved inside Rick's mouth, tickling his throat and the roof of his mouth while preventing him from screaming as it suppressed any sound. The shotgun was knocked out from his hands, it was rested in a pile of grass several feet away, so there was no chance for retrieval. He looked at the beast, scared out of his mind, hoping someone would rescue him. The beast leaned closer, its teeth bared in a savage snarl with its madden eyes peering down at Rick. Gently, the beast started to apply a slow yet gradual pressure, pulling up against the upper jawline of his prey. Rick could feel it like a crowbar levering against a padlock, feeling the hinges of his skull beginning to bend and splinter, causing severe pain. The tears started to flow down his cheek as he prayed to whatever god was watching for salvation. The beast leaned closer, its breath dewing Rick's ear as it whispered:

"I told you this would happen..." growled the beast sinisterly, resembling Finn in a deeper, rustic tone.

At first, it didn't register in Rick's mind, but once it had, he barely had time to react, looking down at the beast with a shocked expression of disbelief. In one fluid motion, Finn ripped off Rick's head and flung the remains into a nearby trashcan. Rick was only conscious for a few minutes, flying a great distance in the air and away from his body. As Rick looked onward, he watched Finn opening the ribcage of his now-headless body. His head cracked against the metal frame of the trashcan as it was left open. It rattled like a bead in a rainmaker, shaking the contents of the garbage. His sight began to darken, covered in filth and blood running down his face from the neck and the fracture that split open on his forehead. Rick couldn't feel anything at this point, and he couldn't even breathe; he could only watch and feel his mind drift away.

As for Finn, he continued eating away at Rick's carcass like a buffet table, taking some joy in this particular meal. This lasted for some time, perhaps a few more minutes, before he sensed something from behind, his ears perking upward and his nose sniffing in the air. His head darted back, his mouth streaming with blood and inners from the corners of his jaw, a bloodlust over his yellow eyes as he stared furiously. He stopped short when he saw it was Freddy, his face washed away of any color, and left with a mortified look as he pointed his gun. There was only one reaction that entered his thoughts as he looked at the beast:

".... Finny?"

Finn was taken aback by Freddy's wild-guess, the accusation weighing down on him even more significantly since he was exposed to the truth. He didn't know how to respond, but he knew he couldn't lay a finger on Freddy, not HIM of all people...

".... I can explain EVERYTHING!"

END OF THE NIGHT

October 27th

The Slasher

It was particularly busy at the store, but fewer and fewer people left as closing time was fast approaching the store. However, it seemed odd to Tim that bags of candy labeled with discounted prices were left in mass quantities, undisturbed on the racks. Tim adjusted his dark-orange wool beanie hat. He rubbed his temples around the side of his forehead in aggravation as he looked to the side, brushing the bangs of his greasy-slick black hair away. Each rack littered across the entire aisle with Christmas decorations, peppermint candy, cheaply-made toys, and greeting cards with reindeer sleighs. They had conquered what was left of the Halloween items, sitting only two of the shelves at the end of the lane. It seemed all of the rest of the shelves from either side were just Christmas, Christmas, and more Christmas. It pissed him off, and his anger was practically seething and visible on his face. He didn't even notice the couple that had just appeared at his checkout line.

"Hey… HEY TIM, you there?" called the voice.

"… HUH, what?" Tim stammered, taken by surprise. His head spun back in place, facing the customers.

"Is this line open, Tim?" questioned Finn, accompanied by Freddy, interlocked by the arms. The other carried the small shopping basket. The two were taking an inventory of hair-care products, fresh vegetables, and some bags of snack-sized candies, among the other items hidden in a pile, brimming at the edges.

"Sorry, the light was on so we assumed you were open now," asked Freddy.

"Oh no, it's open, I'm sorry about that. I guess I wasn't paying attention…" Tim answered, forcing himself to bear an embarrassed grin. He rubbed the back of his neck as he began rolling the items across the scanner and into the bagging area. After the first two or four items, he looked up again with a greater sense of composure.

"Did you find everything okay today, Mr. Zachery?"

"Please, you can call me 'Fred,' and yes, we found more than what we bargained for," Freddy chuckled as he patted Finn's arm affectionally.

"Great, I'm glad to hea-" Tim stopped short as he glanced down at one of the items in his hand. He cringed and, for a moment, froze in his place.

"Oh no," blurted Freddy, "I know that look. Finny, you didn't."

"What? What's wrong?" Finn asked.

Tim shook his head, ringing the box of Christmas lights out onto the register. It read DISCOUNT in red lettering, subtracted from the total amount on the bill.

"Nothing is wrong, Mr. Alexander, just a spasm..." announced Tim.

"And you can call ME 'Finn,' and really, what's up?" asked Finn, pressing the matter further.

"He HATES Christmas," snorted Freddy, gesturing the lights in the loose, transparent bag.

No, I don't, MR. ZACHERY," chuckled Tim, "I'd like to clarify that it's not Christmas I hate, but people were celebrating Christmas outside of December... you know, like in October...."

"When it should be Halloween, I get it... it's not even Thanksgiving yet," Freddy replied, rolling his eyes and then pinching Finn's cheek, "Why didn't you tell me you put this in our basket?"

"I didn't see why not, it was a bargain and it doesn't hurt to plan ahead," answered Finn, looking up innocently at Freddy.

"Because we haven't celebrated Halloween yet. It's only five days away, can't we have the Halloween spirit before we move to Christmas mode?" argued Tim, halfway completed with the scanning and bagging of the items.

"Well... it's not like Halloween is an ACTUAL holiday through..." claimed Finn with a sarcastic tone in his voice.

Tim sighed, not wanting to complain further to such friendly customers, while Freddy stared with a gaping mouth and raised an eyebrow. His hand shot across his face, covering the dramatic gasp escaping his lips as he began to glare at Finn.

Tim knew it was an actual holiday after the history report he wrote as an extra-credit assignment. It only seemed right, being his favorite holiday and his family being strongly supportive of their Celtic heritage. On the other hand, Freddy knew Halloween had an enormous impact than that from recent experiences:

"Oh man, you should NOT be talking, especially what happened last night," remarked Freddy, shaking his head in disappointment.

Finn winced, growing cold and clammy instantly, "Why would you bring that up now in front of people? And what does that have to do with anything?"

"We'll talk about it at the house," muttered Freddy, corking that discussion for later. He quickly looped one arm around Finn while grabbing the few bags of groceries with the other. He gave a glance at Tim and smiled broadly with a wink of the eye:

"I'll give him an extra earful for you when we do get home, give him the lesson on Halloween spirit. How much do we owe you?"

"Oh," Fin looked at the cashier screen, dialing the total over the tiny keyboard, "it comes up to $31.13."

They exchanged the money, with folded twenties, and Tim gave back in singles and loose change. Finn merely waited for Freddy to finish, staring out into space and avoiding further conversation while fidgeting awkwardly like a child waiting for his parent. When everything was in order, Freddy smiled as he started to stroll out with Finn. Finn gave a nervous smile and a short wave to Tim for appearance. He tried to hurry along with Freddy in tow:

"I'll see you back in history class tomorrow, Tim..." Finn called back, just as the two made their way to the store's entrance. Tim, however, could overhear a bit before they left and were cut off, "...oh calm down, Finny. It's not like anyone would believ-"

They disappeared, and Tim stood there, rolling his eyes and slightly grumbling underneath his breath. He thought to himself, Mr. Zachery was one of the few teachers he liked at school. Tim pulled out his phone, killing time before the next customer.

"OH, and Tim?" called Freddy, his head sprung out from the side of the entrance in a comical way as if poking out from a curtain. Tim's head shot back up in surprise, away from the screen, the phone nearly falling out of his hand. His eyes pinpointed at the entrance doors and onto Freddy's beaming smile:

"… Merry Christmas!" hollered Freddy, giggling as he saw Tim's face trying to stop the contortion and halfway grin.

"Thank you, MR. ZACHERY!"

#

It would be a few short hours following the encounter with Freddy and Finn, and Tim relatively spent the time watching the store empty out. There was no particular need to assist further shoppers or occupy the cashier again for Tim. Before long, the store had officially closed for the night, and the only one left was Tim. The store required that a rotating night shift be given to one employee. Each day of the week would fall onto every employee at last once. This time, Tim would be required to oversee the stock, manage the shelves and clean any leftover mess. He would assess any damage, turn off all electronics and lighting, then close and lock up at last. He didn't mind too much; Tim did it reasonably quickly and required minimal effort. It was all mechanical at a certain point, and repetition had created a rhythmic motion that carried Tim with ease.

Soon, he had completed all his evening chores except for one area. In an aisle he had intentionally avoided for as long as he could, he no longer could for fear of reprimanding from his supervising employer— the Christmas Aisle.

With reluctance, he scuffled through the hallway, eyeing the shelves with contempt and nausea, fighting the urge to trash the items into the garbage. He could blame it on vandalism by students; it'd be passable considering the recent events deemed as pranks rather than actual crimes. Just some bratty, spoiled kids that want attention and thrills. The problem was, however, the security cameras and their footage. They catch nearly everything, and it'd be hard to tamper for some time. It wasn't like he could play old footage or something over a loop. He didn't have that type of expertise or master plan like in the movies. That and the paperwork would be tedious, keeping the story straight and all while managing the vanishing act of the stock in ledgers.

In any event, he didn't spend much effort or thought into his search and nearly reached the end of the hall. It was disappointing. He had partially hoped something awful would've occurred that would've let him blameless and taken action to "rectify" the supposed problem. He, however, found nothing amiss and decided he accounted for in the end. As he made his way, he came across a section with the snowmen lined up in rows, almost as if they were awaiting their marching orders for war. Tim stopped at the end of the line, staring down at one particular snowman.

It had an icy chill to its demeanor for some odd reason. A bulbous, hollow shell that rose to Tim's height, lumbering over his skinny body. Its black-coal eyes were dull and menacing, expressing no warmth in its face intended for the young audiences it served to please. The long orange carrot nose pointed outward jaggedly like a serrated knife. It wore its cheap, manufactured smile embedded into the white snowy face like an imprint from a foot. Its thick arms, packed with plastic snow, huddled the broomstick between a fat elbow and wrapped its red-gloved hands by the shat. And to top it all off, the black stove hat was almost comically misshaped and the wrong size as it teetered on the head. It made the snowman appear like a homeless beggar than a jolly old soul.

Along the neck, a red, plastic scarf hid the coal buttons partially, something that always seemed unnatural. If the eyes were also coals, wouldn't that also make the buttons the eyes, or would it be the other way around? It was an argument that bore similarities to another questionable predicament. Whether a gingerbread man was made of a house or if the house was made of the man. Tim chuckled at such a stupid idea with all of this reasoning, taking too much thought into it. As absurd as it sounded in his head, however, it reminded him of Halloween again.

Despite this brief feeling, these Christmas creeps were making him slightly enraged. He couldn't stand it anymore and didn't care about the security cameras. He drew in a wad of mucus and saliva. He spat across the face of that particular nasty-looking snowman between those soulless black eyes. It was actually an impressive shot, if not vulgar.

He gave a short scuff and concluded his rounds, making his way back to the backroom of the store. The exit was in sight, and he was a few steps away from the door when he heard a sound, like something skidding across the tiled pavement, erupt behind him. He didn't turn around immediately. He waited. Slowly, he turned and didn't see anything. He looked off to the sides then ahead and found a small pile of white crumbs scattered across the ground by the snowmen. Only when he looked closer that he saw one of them was missing from the rack. Tim tossed his head, rolling his eyes and annoyed, he cried out across the store so the unknown entity could hear him as far as possible:

"WHOEVER IS DOING THIS, I'M NOT IN THE MOOD! I'm calling the police and then I'm locking the building up so COME OUT NOW!"

No reply.

He cursed underneath his breath as he wasn't bluffing. Still, he'd rather not avoid any trouble with the police and his supervisors. He decided to go back into the employee office; for now, he could use the security cameras to find the culprit within the building effectively. As he strolled around, he heard a rustle, a sort of commotion occurring in a nearby aisle. It sounded as if some heavy and metal had fallen onto the floor in a heap.

"Nope, not falling for that..." he called back while picking up the pace.

He knew that's how all the horror movies started: someone "investigates" a noise, then shit hits the fan. And while he knew this wasn't a horror movie, he wasn't going to play dumb for any reason.

As he entered the faculty room, he locked the door behind him for safe measure, sat on the desk chair, and wheeled himself over to the computer with the security monitors. An array of screens lit up, recording the live footage of the entire store. He knew to rely on these cameras as they were new and up-to-date. They could cover the whole interior of the building as well as outside. Tim glanced at each monitor screen, scrutinizing each footage before moving onto the next:

Camera 1, cleared...

Camera 2, cleared...

Camera 3, cleared...

Camera 4, cleared…

Camera 5, clea-wait…

Tim backtracked and peered at Camera 4 again. He recalled that that camera surveyed the gardening and hardware aisle. There, standing in the middle of the aisleway, was one of the snowman decorations. In its snow-white hands, it wasn't a broomstick but a shining-new ax lugged over the crook of its arms, similarly as it did with the broomstick before. And it just stood there, in that same pose, with its head unnaturally lifted up, staring at the camera with those black eyes.

Tim cocked an eyebrow, then took a microphone that connected the desk to the intercom of the stores. He turned it on and spoke into it, making sure he pronounced the message clearly:

"Very impressive, but you're going to have to pay for that snowman… you better just come clear and face me, I'm coming over now."

Tim walked out of the office, taking the time to lock the door behind him and hold on to the keys afterward. Once done, he tried to be silent as he moved to the other side of the store stealthy. He didn't see anyone from the other side of the hall, so he planned to "race" to the other side and quietly inspect each aisle as he made his way to the garden and hardware section. One by one, he didn't see anyone, and once he was at the foot of the department, at last, he hesitated to continue further. Tim could try the other aisles and see if he could catch the culprit in the act or try his luck with the snowman. He shrugged his shoulders. It seemed the safer bet and might draw the prankster out. Slowly, he crept behind the snowman until he looked at its backside and its lopsided hat taunting Tim. He inspected the snowman, trying to see if someone tempered anything other than the ax, but it seemed normal. He gave a gentle nudge and no reaction as expected, but he couldn't take much more.

Tim turned his head to the side, hoping to see a snickering child huddled at the end of the aisle or some teenager with an amateur camera in hand. He found none, which only ticked him off. He turned back with the snowman gone altogether, which didn't register with his brain. His eyes swiped to both sides of the aisle way, then behind him again. But it remained the fact that the snowman had vanished for sure.

This movement was too elaborate of a prank, and it was beginning to scare Tim.

As soon as he drew his breath again, his heart began to convulse as music blasted the intercom without warning. Tim fell onto the floor, holding his chest, then peering upward to the ceiling with a feverish look in his eyes. It was a Christmas melody, once a cheery, happy tune seemed dark and mournful in an abandoned building. Quickly, his hands fumbled at his waist, trying to find the keyring that should've stayed attached to his belt. He couldn't find it. In that instance, he came to the logical conclusion that there was more than one person. The first was stationed at the aisle to move the snowman while pickpocketing the keys, then handed them off to the partner so that he or she could play the music from the office. That was the only way it all made sense to Tim, and it slowly calmed him down, and he could feel the air return to his lungs again.

Tim raced out of the aisle and headed towards the office until he nearly stumbled, trying to grab onto the handle of the door. Amidst the booming Christmas song, Tim pounded on the door and screamed: "IT'S OVER! If you have nowhere to go so you don't open RIGHT now, I'm calling the police and having them break the door down!"

Tim didn't want to wait any longer, taking a few steps away from the door and reaching into his pocket for his phone. Then the music stopped, causing Tim to halt, look up at the ceiling with a shocked look, and then at the door again with a pompous sneer.

Tap- tap- tap

A sharp chime echoed through the hall like the raping of a pointed edge. It was something similar to a pin dropping on the floor, repeating like a rhythm.

Tap- tap- tap-

Tim turned his head to the other side of the store. It was past the milk and eggs and towards the freezer section. By the right-side corner of the store, where the emergency exit was located, sat the snowman at last.

Tap- tap- tap-

It was only looking at the snowman did he see the ax tapping on the tile over and over. The arm of the snowman rising and lowering the handle so smoothly. As Tim looked onward, holding his breath, the cold-sweating beading down his face, and the hairs on his neck standing on ends, he could see the arm clearer. It was broken off in several places from the casted plastic, cracked in a jigsaw to allow the movement.

Tap- tap- tap-

Tim looked up and stared at the snowman's distorted face, no longer smiling gently but broken into a fallen scowl across its jagged jawline. The wad of mucus and saliva trickling down its nose like solidifying glue. The snowman stopped, snapped its arm back with both hands on the handle, and began sliding across the floor towards Tim, gaining speed from a slow crawl to a bustling engine. Tim didn't bother to think anymore. He sped faster than the snowman, heading towards the garden and hardware section again.

Tim ducked towards the aisle abruptly, hiding from the sight of the snowman. It was almost at the end of the hall to where he was. The snowman was at the edge of the aisle way, prepared to cut Tim off with its ax swung in the air and ready to swing back at the boy's vulnerable neck. The very blade was inches away, reflecting the face of the boy's mortified expression.

And Tim swung the ax, and it hit its mark, severing the neck clean with a crack. The head went flying off and landed on the pavement as the body scrambled onto the floor alongside. The head slid a few inches, forming a trail of white powder and plastic fragments with the snowman's face gripped with agony across its now-animating face. Tim stood there, shaking like a leaf in the wind. He dropped the ax on the floor beside his feet. He counted himself lucky, it was the last ax left on the shelves, and it had done its job.

Tim didn't wait any longer. He didn't care what or who was in that snowman. The snowman was still clawing its way to Tim and thus convinced him it was a threat. He acted accordingly: it was self-defense, so prank or not, he wasn't going to stay any longer. He leaped across the snowman's body before it could regain the hold of its ax. He managed to kick the snowman's head like a hockey player with its puck to the goalie post, sliding across the floor to the end of the hall. Tim continued running, ignoring the employee office that remained locked down, and sprinted out of the emergency exit.

The alarm went off, the siren blaring out from the outside speakers and the red lights accompanying the protocol as it blinked on and off. Tim shut the door behind him and pinned his body against the metal frame as if to hold off whatever was inside the store. He heard the click from the lock and knew he wouldn't be able to get back in. He was free. The adrenaline in his blood kept him warm against the chill in the air, the frosty wind that sped across his body. He fell to his knees, his hands slide across the metal, with one hand wrapped around his throat as he stared nervously at the black paved road. At this point, Tim was hyperventilating and losing his mind; he only wanted to get out desperately. The sickening effect in his stomach wrecked his body. It churned and ripped into his insides like the blades of a blender. It felt him minced and liquidated, but he couldn't help laughing. He was free.

With a shaking hand, from frost or fright, Tim reached to his pocket to find the keys to his car. He couldn't decide whether to stay in the car and drive back home, stay up all night until the break of dawn unless someone came for me. God, he hoped it'd be the police...

Taptaptaptaptaptaptaptaptaptaptaptaptaptaptaptaptaptaptaptaptaptap taptaptaptaptaptaptap...

Tim's blood froze when he heard the sound again, but it was a thunderous chorus, almost like a call of battle. He knew it was the axes, and he knew where they were from, but he prayed to whoever was listening that he was wrong. He didn't want to see another snowman...

He started to cry, and he didn't want to look because deep down, he knew what he'd find regardless of his hopes or reasoning. He turned his head, tears sliding down his cheeks, and found himself surrounded by snowman, tapping their axes in perfect unison against the road. Each snowman stood in lines, shoulder-to-shoulder, cutting off any attempt to escape by Tim. He huddled towards the door; he couldn't even see past the snowman, nor did he try to find his car in the hopes of spearheading past them. He didn't try to reason or talk to whatever were these things. All he did was cry and mumbled to himself:

"It's... not... Christmas...."

The tapping stopped, and the sound of sliding plastic began to creep towards Tim. His eyes darted up, and he could see each face of every snowman, twisted in an outstretched smile ripped across the snow-white surface like shards of glass breaking off. They were all smiling as Tim began to scream, but the sirens slowly drowned it out with the light of the security alarm flickering on and off.

END OF THE NIGHT

October 28th

The Snake

"In short," said Ms. Claymore to the class, "the police are investigating the incident concerning Mr. Timothy Jenkins.

She paused, waiting for a reaction before continuing: "And if I find out that it was one of my students that was involved with this despicable "prank," you can expect consequences."

She looked around the classroom at each table, gauging their reactions and behavior, but she found little to none as expected. The few students that were paying attention stared emptily into space with only some pretense of retention. Some others were talking amongst themselves quietly while the other half were on their phones. They weren't even trying to hide them underneath the tables; they simply texted and scrolled away at their screens. Ms. Claymore sighed disappointedly, trying to keep it on track and emphasize the situation:

"You could TRY and sympathize with Tim, you know. It was because of this "prank" that he's in the hospital and exhibiting some post-traumatic stres-"

She was interrupted by a cackle, followed by snickering from the older students that rippled through the classroom. Then simmered to discussion amongst each other at and across their tables. Ms. Claymore clapped her hands to get their attention like she was addressing a dog, attempting to talk over them:

"WITH HOW THINGS ARE PROGRESSING, we cannot stress caution enough, this could happen to anyone else. Please be mindful and careful out there, for your sake at least…."

She pleaded with her class earnestly, hoping they received the message. Still, to no avail, the students had kept talking over her;

they had all decided the discussion was over. She conceded in defeat, moving along to her lesson plan for the day and projecting the directions onto the digital whiteboard. They were finishing up with their clay sculptures, an activity that garnered some participation at first. Today, they would turn over their final products to the kiln, fired and cooked until they harden at last. Each student had crafted different pieces, bowels, pots, jugs, boxes, cups with the typical shape. In contrast, others had attempted unique forms and models.

One peculiar student completed her creation, a star pupil in the Art Department with exceptional talent with such earthly materials. Her name was Diana Embar, a skilled student in the class and favored by all professors for her work. She specializes in clay and stone carvings, but she typically works with wire sculptures, metalwork, and oil paintings. When she's not at work in the studio, she's occupied by the Theatre Department, volunteering for positions like scenery, stagehands, electronics, and sound. She's even acted in small parts in plays and musical numbers when needed. However, she'd never admitted to enjoying the experiences and preferred behind the scenes. On the surface, she seemed to be an excellent student, shown in the limelight on college campus.

She worked tirelessly on her sculptures, allowed to stay in the secluded yet tranquil workspace separated from the class. It was a large studio room that held all of the materials and equipment in storage which granted her all the supplies she could need, particularly the kiln. Her olive-skinned hands were deep into the cold, wet mound of clay, shaping its form into a Greek vase. She was interested in attempting to recreate their ancient process as it was a part of her heritage while maintaining the modern spinning wheel. Later, she hoped to illustrate a tale using black acrylic paint with articulated fine-hair brushes like depicted in history textbooks. It was almost done...

"How's it coming along?" erupted a voice behind Diana, sitting on the stool as she whisked her vase in her hands.

"Crap!" exclaimed Diana, slamming her foot onto the pedal of the pottery wheel from a frightful reaction.

The wheel spun out of control at high speed, her fingers clenched up and dug into the clay. By a stroke of luck, she instinctively lifted off the pedal and back her hands off like it was scalding hot. By that time, however, it was already too late. The vase had spiraled into a corkscrew formation which steadily concaved from its misbalanced weight. It was practically a mound of clay again, but this wasn't too difficult for her to salvage and make anew. Diana took a hand, dripped into a small cup of water, and moisten the clay once more. She turned her head, looking up at her assailant while maintaining her seat. As expected, it was a horrified Jocelyn, her only best friend, her hands covering her mouth.

"Relax Jocy, I can fix it easily." Diana said reassuringly, already starting from the structure's base without even looking at what she was doing.

"But... I mean, I'm still sorry... you know I would never..." stammered Jocelyn, pleading and almost watering up with anxious tears.

"Duh, I know that so don't worry, I'm not mad at all. It gives me the time to improve," she said, easing her grip and relaxing the shoulders, "Besides, I'm done."

"Wait, really?"

Jocelyn looked over Diana's shoulder and saw that she had finished the job indeed. The vase stood as if nothing had happened; it seemed almost symmetrical and better than before. Diana wiped the corners of her beading forehead with a forearm, and some clay still managed to cling to her violet-dyed hair. She turned her to inspect the work and then back to Jocelyn with a proud, beaming smile.

"What do you think?" she asked.

"It's amazing... not just the piece," she confessed, pulling back her bangs covering her face, "You're the best artist in this university, how do you do it?"

Diana blushed a shade of pink, brimming from cheek to cheek when she heard her say that. She wanted to tell Jocelyn how she felt and describe to her what her inspiration was. Or better yet, something more personal that she's been hiding for some time. But it wasn't the time for that now, she thought, and her face sullied into a sort of grimace.

"I don't know, I guess it's partially talent. Maybe after a while, my hands just take over for me like a motion or reflex," she replied, resuming her work with the final additions. She took one of the carving scalpels and traced two lines to make a section between the opening rim and partially near the base. She accomplished this by pressing the pedal to the wheel to create a perfect seamless contour. This step would serve as the space for the painted illustration on the Greek vase, like a frame for the picture, once she completed the first firing process to ensure it was a solid piece. Once Diana completed that process, she took a wire and slipped it underneath the base to separate the vase from the metal wheel surface. The moist clay practically glued it to the wheel. After she pried the clay off, she gingerly moved it to the kiln and set it down but not before engraving her initials into the underbelly of the vase's base.

All the while, Jocelyn watched in a patient and attentive manner over Diana's shoulder as if eagerly noting at her craft like a dotting apprentice. Diana welcomed the gaze. She always felt safe, confident, and appreciated for who she was in Jocelyn's eyes; she did not have to hide anything and be herself, especially from her. Well, she still had to hide a few yet essential secrets of herself...

As soon as she closed the door to the kiln, however, an unwelcome gaze appeared at the doorway and announced himself obnoxiously, cutting off the serene silence:

"How are you ladies doing on this lovely day?" chimed Theodore, leaning past the doorway and sticking his head out.

Theodore was of average height and built, and he was an exceedingly good student in terms of the grade point average. Or so he tried to convince his teachers and peers. Diana knew he had cheated and stolen work from others and covered his tracks quickly. Due to his lack of artistry and creativity, the thievery was apparent. Still, it made him frustrated and envious of Diana's skill. He would often just sit at his desk, scrolling his phone or talking to a group of students until Diana had finished her work and left it unguarded in the late hours. Otherwise, he hid his envy and wrath behind his handsome features and charisma that compensated for his failings vastly. The typical popular boy that all the other students gushed around to the pinnacle of cliché film-troupe. They would all try to get him to join their clubs, sports, and their fraternities as if to become a name-brand supporting a celebrity spokesperson. As one may come to expect from this, he was immensely vain to an additional fault.

He strolled through the doorway, his eyes darting around the room, but Diana had already closed the kiln and stood a few feet away from it. Jocelyn stood silently, her attention focused on Theodore, attempting not to look out and over to the kiln to help Diana conceal her secret. Theodore sensed the tension and picked up their subtle signals, smirking as he glanced at the locked kiln with a deduced assumption. He leaned onto the kiln's side and shifted towards Diana:

"What's your next masterpiece, Diana?" asked Theodore, "Can I take a peek?"

"I've already submitted my work to Mrs. Claymore, she's documented the work so it won't get "lost" again. You can ask her; she might even let you take notes."

"Woah, that almost sounds like an accusation. That's not towards me, is it?" Theodore said mockingly, his smile still cemented on his lips.

"Not at all, I'm just stating the facts. I'm sorry you can't see it now," Diana said coldly.

"Then what about you, Jocy?" he said, turning his gaze.

Jocelyn shook nervously at that moment; a chill ran down her hazelnut skin, making the hairs stand on ends. She looked away, biting her bottom lip as she hastily tried to find the right words:

"I-I finished painting... with the oils, that is... a-a-a- few days ago..." she spoke like a broken needle on a record player."I'm allowed to work on other pieces... or watch the other students... in my spare time... as-as long as it doesn't interfere with their work...."

"Wow, you must have a lot of free time then," he answered with an exaggerated sense of surprise, "you're always seem to be with Diana these days. If you need something to do, I could use some help with my work.... or I could give you some hands-on lessons..."

At that point, Diana walked over and stood between Theodore and Jocelyn, intercepting their discussion and blocking his leering view of her. Diana stared at him, an emotionless and indifferent expression on her face as she crossed her arms as if she were staring at a bug on the floor she was about to smash against her heel. Theodore could sense the unrelenting and unforgiving judgment in her eyes. And it made him cringe for a short duration.

"She's already agreed to help me with some of my other work, maybe another time?"

Theodore stared blankly at Diana, looking past her and waiting for any reaction from Jocelyn herself. There was only a long pause of silence, and so he rolled his eyes and started to make his way out but not before having the last word:

"I can see you're both EXTREMELY busy," he replied with a snarky sarcasm, "I'll see myself out. You both have a great day."

As he left the room, Jocelyn gave a heavy exhale as if she held her breath for the entire time. Her tension lessened, relaxing her body and slumping over slightly. Diana, however, felt like she was still walking across eggshells and could not ease down from her temper. She sped to the door, locking it shut, and then facing Jocelyn:

"That frickening creep, "few pointers," my ***! I know e-x-a-c-t-l-y which little "pointer" he'd like to use," she scowled, extending her tiny pinky-finger in measurement. She wiggled it in an obscuring manner between her legs for inappropriate humor yet added effect.

"Stop, he might hear you," Jocelyn laughed, waving her arms at Diana in a pleading manner.

"Good, he needs to get off his eff-ing high-horse, the two-faced, lying sack of...," replied Diana, flinging her middle finger at the door.

"Okay okay, I get it," she agreed with Diana, laughing it off.

Diana checked the contents of the kiln before she would lock the door completely. An industrial kiln served as a large furnace with a vast amount of space accompanied by several shelves for smaller pieces. She noticed several other projects, the shelves filled with bowels, pots, pans, and other typical pieces of artwork found in any art classroom. As she walked further in, she discovered her clay pieces placed on the right side near a bottom shelf behind the steel door as per usual. This decision was intentional as it was a blind spot when you entered at first glance so that Theodore couldn't find them so easily. With this, the documentation, and the signatures on the work, she did all she could to keep her artwork safe from prying hands. The only thing she could do was transport the artwork as quickly from out of the kiln afterward.

Before she left, she looked onward to the corner of the kiln, taking inventory of her last and more extensive piece of work. It was a life-sized statue, modeled after Greek style but bared a more modern appearance, a male figure neutered without offending gentile and stripped of any clothing. He had only his wild short hair with equally-rugged looks such as a crude nose and large eyebrows, prominent lips that had a low scowl, and small beady eyes. He did, however, carry an open book in one arched arm. At the same time, the other handheld an apple, using authentic items as props to illustrate meaning in learning and education. Due to her unparalleled talent and skill, she was recognized for her diligent work; the school elected to pay a commission for an art piece from her. This artwork would feature in their establishment for a set amount of time near the front entrance. It was, as they said, to inspire the students to strive towards learning and achievements. Another reason why Theodore wanted the credit for her artwork, it meant a line of revenue for his expensive tastes.

But this piece, she thought, was something he wouldn't want credit for if he knew.

She finished her rounds, locked the door behind her, and made her way back to her table, where she found Jocelyn waiting for her, to her delight. Jocelyn was sitting on the table, brimming with an excited smile and swinging her legs like a child on a playground, wanting to see what Diana would work on next:

"I've got a few more commissions," Diana replied, setting her table for the next project, "you can stay and watch, but I'll be here until after-school... I can ask Ms. Claymore if you can stay behind through."

"That'd be cool, but I think I need to talk to another professor about a missing assignment so I'll meet up with you later, would that be okay?"

"Oh yeah, I'll be done by then... I think," Diana answered, uncertain of herself as she contemplated on the list of projects she had for this week due for the month.

She'd make it work.

#

Later that night, Diana had kept working long after the other students had left the building during dismissal, with only a few staff members roaming the hallways. The staff dimmed the lights per protocol, saving energy but permitting late-night students to work for a set amount of time. Diana worked under a small, flickering fixture above her, not distracted by any noise or sight. She knew, however, that she'd have to finish up soon. For a brief minute, she stopped to breathe evenly and wipe her brow from the strain of concentration, looking around to see if she would have her expected visitor. There was, however, no one else but herself and the statues that filled the room. Disappointed but not discouraged, she shrugged her shoulders and decided this was an excellent point to stop her work. She could continue tomorrow or perhaps bring some with her home.

There was series of footsteps approaching the doorway, and her immediate thought was Jocelyn. She became eager to show her work again:

"Hey Jocy, you're just in time, I was just about to lea-"

"Jocelyn, huh? That explains a lot now...."

She shuddered at the voice, regretted ever jumping to the conclusion before the person showed himself. Theodore appeared through the doorway, smiling from ear to ear as the lights continued to flicker ominously, casting shadows over his face like a harlequin. He took a few steps forward, inching closer to where Diana was standing by her workbench; she had felt a sliver of doubt and fear. She had already recovered, feeling nothing towards him. Still, she maintained a relaxed cover as she placed the tools back to their respective places. She didn't even look at him as she prepared to leave:

"I told you, I've already told Ms. Claymore about the incident and recorded all of my work...."

"Right, and I'll admit, I was coming over initially to steal some of your work," he confessed, moving in closer.

"Wait, you just admitted tha-"

"But I've had a change of heart, there's something else that caught my attention. Something that I think is worth the trouble," Theodore interrupted, slithering closer and closer behind her as she turned away from growing discomfort.

He was only a few inches away from her now. She had her belongings in her backpack and gripped the straps tightly. She prepared herself to slam her bag against his smug face. Then run towards the entrance and find a professor other staff member, as any normal, threatened woman would do in the situation. It made her skin crawl at how close he was to her, and she could feel his nauseous breath against her neck as he stood there behind her. But she knew she had to keep control; she couldn't lash out erratically yet.

"I think it'd be a greater achievement if I got a lesbian to go out with me, it'd say a lot about me turning her bisexual, don't you think?"

"What," she broke into dilated speech before regaining composure, "makes you think I'd say yes to that?"

She tried to contain her laugh as not to provoke him, but she could barely pull through; she couldn't help be both amazed and shocked by his man-handling ego. How could he think so big of himself when he was capable of doing so little? She theorized that it was overcompensating for a near-confirmed deformity, one that some might say was a disability in some regions of growth and reproduction. She covered her mouth, waiting for his answer:

"Or else I'll tell Jocy what you REALLY are...."

She flinched, and the laughter replaced with something more dark and tragic. She held herself, standing strong against the violator, but a part of her shrunk as well. There was brief quiet-stillness between them, and Theodore scoffed under his breath as he continued:

"You don't ACTUALLY she feels the same way as you do? And once she finds out that you're a bitch, you won't have her as a CLOSE friend anymore. And that will spread quick around college, you'll be an outcast even more than usual...."

He placed a hand on her shoulder, but she wasn't concerned anymore. She had flipped her switch and sharpened her instincts to a razor-edge like a dagger waiting in the dark. She was ready to strike in due time. He droned on:

"So why don't you be a "normal" girl and do what you're told, once it's over and the word is on the street, you'll be able to keep being friends with Jocy... once I'm done with her next, that is...."

He couldn't see past her shoulder, but he wasn't paying attention to begin with at all. More so, he was focused on moving along to caressing her waist, left to his repulsive thoughts and defiling imagination. It gave her time, however, to remove her contact lenses from her eyes quickly. She placed them in a protective case as she prepared herself for what was to come next. She knew what he was initially implying, but she took it as a threat. Her mother had told her that she was allowed to defend herself and sweep away the evidence if anyone found out her *particular* secret. He continued:

"That's alright with you, right? We WON'T have any more problems after tonight, right?"

He waited on her reply, and she nodded in agreement. There wouldn't be any more problems after she commenced her last art project for the night. She closed her eyes, turning to face Theodore. He chuckled, thinking he had won at last, and she could imagine his grotesque smile, stretched past his lips and up towards his eyes like some jeering clown. She was happy. It would be a perfect addition and a lasting impression. She opened her eyes, Theodore witnessing her hidden secret, but not the one he had expected.

Theodore merely stood there, unmoving and seemingly unfazed, his features frozen on his body. His mind reeled, trying to understand what had happened. He could only stare at her, trying to see if her eyes were natural or if it was supposed to be a tricky prank. A few seconds had passed, and he couldn't feel his muscles. He tried to move, but he couldn't even wiggle his fingers, still hovering over her waist until she moved away from his grasp. She placed her contact lenses back, hiding those emerald-green, silted basilisk eyes behind the dull, dark blue irises again. She rolled up her dyed hair into a bun, using a ribbon tied from her neck before she addressed the petrified Theodore:

"I'm not JUST a lesbian, I'm part gorgon on my mother's side. And since you never pay attention in art-history class, a gorgon is a "mythical" Greek creature that was part human and part snake, like Medusa. And if you haven't figured it out, a gorgon has the ability to turn people to stone by eye-sight, that's why you can't move...."

As she rolled up her sleeves, she made her way back to the kiln, unlocking the latch and disappearing into the dark cavern. Theodore couldn't look behind him; he became transfixed into looking out in front of him with that stone-cold expression. He could only hear her move the pots and sculptures around the shelves and floor, scraping across the concrete surface with the dry, gritty clay. Then there was silence, only for Diana to appear face-to-face swiftly, sending a terrifying wave through him in a sudden torrent.

"It's not like in the stories through, it takes a longer time to eventually become stone since the bloodline has diluted over the centuries but you'll remain paralyzed for now on. But consequentially," Diana trailed off, beginning to take off Theodore's jacket with a pair of scissors.

She snipped the seams around his shoulders, dismantling the patches of fabric covering his body. At first, he was bewildered, then resumed his terror, realizing that this wasn't a trick or prank. His mind raced at what she was planning on next, undressed and slowly becoming bare in front of Diana. Luckily for both of them, she had stopped short and left him with only his undershirt and boxers. The discarded scraps were tossed into a black garbage bag, tying a knot and enclosing the clothing within. Soon, placed on a small two-wheel chart, Diana pushed him forward, speaking behind his ear with a forked tongue lashing against a corner:

"You'll still be conscious throughout the process, and still be able to feel everything."

This statement seemed to resonate with him, and it only took a few moments to decipher her meaning as she propped him inside the middle of the kiln. He started to tremble, trying to escape with an ever-rising sense of demise and fear, but he could merely make an inch. He tried looking back, an attempt to plead with Diana or buy time for someone to rescue him from this deranged monster. But she turned him around, facing her with the doorway blocked. He could see the light glowing brightly around her outline. Desperately, he tried to make sounds, emit inaudible words from his glasgow smile. He couldn't even change the expression in his eyes, trying to water the corners to resemble tears to appeal to her remaining humanity.

All she did was snap his limbs into place, Theodore reeling in agony as he felt his bones shattered and forced into position like a hail of stones pummeled him. He couldn't speak, but he managed to grit his teeth and utter a muffled scream that fell into a moan once she had concluded the reconstruction. In the end, Theodore remained poised as if he was holding something to his eye level. One leg extended at the front while the other behind him, his other hand joyously in the air. However, he couldn't tell this, and she left him with no clue about the purpose of this pose. She looked at him, directly at his eyes, with a forbearance of disdain but then, washed away into a boastful smile, spewing a forked-tongue with bated venom dripping at the ends:

"I think I'll give you a mask to hold, something Venetian and clown-like, maybe I'll call it *The Burning Fool....*"

Theodore started to hyperventilate and couldn't think straight and began to scream more of his muffled cries. But Diana had already made her way to the door, only taking a moment to look back one last time. Then she closed the door, and the kiln became pitch-black, only hearing the latch close and lock snapping into place in the end. He held his breath, and soon, little flames started to pop out from all parts of the kiln's interior like an array of candles lit in a chapel. They grew larger and larger, the flame turning from a subtle red to a blistering white.

Diana didn't bother to stay and watch his remains become charred-flesh, they would become stone shortly afterwards; she had to leave the scene of the crime as soon as possible. She began to take a final inspection of her table, looking around for any pieces of evidence. In the morning, she'd come in early to the college and begin cleaning the area with potent chemicals on the pretense that she "forgot" to do so before she left the previous night. This would be a final deterrent to avoid any residue (fingerprints, blood, nails, etc.) before police got involved like in the other incidents. When she felt secure, she took a grab at the trash bag containing Theodore's clothes.

"Oh, hey Diana, are you leaving now?"

She felt her skin become clammy and icy-cold, but she attempted to maintain her composure as she turned to address Jocelyn, hauling the garbage bag over her shoulder:

"Yeah, sorry you missed it but I was just finishing up. Do you mind helping me with my backpack? I have to take these used materials to the dumpster around the back."

"Oh, sure. I wanted to walk back with you anyway," Jocelyn said nervously as she awkwardly dove to the backpack.

"Cause of my intoxicatingly-enchanting presence?" Diana laughed, moving in front of the simmering kiln and blocking its door.

"Sure… and what's been happening lately," she giggled, carrying the backpack in her hand, "you heard Ms. Claymore, it's not safe to go alone at night."

"Aw, you do care," she smiled, looping an arm around Jocelyn and hurrying their way out of the art supplies and classroom. Soon, they were a reasonable distance away from the kiln and going down the stairs towards the back entrance.

"Actually," Jocelyn mumbled, fidgeting around the straps of the backpack, "are you… are you free tomorrow night?"

"Wh- um…" Diana shuttered, surprised while grateful for changing the subject, "Yeah, I'm free, why?"

"Well, my family is going out to a pumpkin patch, and we… I… was wondering if you… wanted to come… and carve some jack-o-lanterns…."

"Like, a date?" she asked, hoping but then retracting her words, "I mean, as a family date, do you think that'd be okay?"

"Well, I mean, my mom suggested it… she wanted to meet you… cause I talk about you a lot," she blurted, suddenly regretting having said that out loud as she blushed cherry red.

"Yeah, that'd be cool," Diana accepted, turning a tomato-red herself, thinking to herself that everything was going to turn out better.

And the image of Theodore, along with his fate, began to fade from her memory and conscience. She had won the battle and would continue fighting a war, all for the sake of rescuing her Helen of Troy.

END OF THE NIGHT

October 29th

The Pumpkin

It was a glorious morning, the nourishing sunlight gently shining upon his face and stirring from his restful slumber at last. He took it all in as he stayed nestled in his flowery bed, as soft as a patch of newly stacked hay on the farm. Aroused and awakened, he looked across and off to the sides to see the rest of his younger siblings sleeping in their soft beds. It felt incredible, surrounded by his family after so many had left and gone. A part of him didn't wish to wake his brothers and sisters. It was, however, a new day, and all needed to be attended to and accounted for in the end. With some reluctance, he awoke the others and greeted by a chorus of whining chatter.

All amongst the farm, there was more energy in the fields than usual. He looked around, and more and more, it seemed something was going to happen today. Something big. He heard giggling and awe in their whispers as gossip spread across the community like an entangling vine from the younger children. The grapevine stated that some visitors would be entering the farm. For what reason or cause and effect, it seemed unknown. It was fortuitous luck that he knew a good source of knowledge within an ear-shot distance and so turned to speak with his grandfather. One of the many in their large family, this particular overgrown vegetable, wrinkled and nearly withered from his time on Earth, was visible in his sunken expression. He had seen and heard much in his extended lifetime. However, on this particular day, his grandfather seemed more bedridden, almost sickly to the point of collapse, and deeply troubled than before. His grandfather seemed to be beside himself or deep in thought. Once approached, his grandfather seemed more so:

"Is something wrong?" he asked his grandfather.

"Wrong? Perhaps, I won't know until later tonight but I know why you'd be talking to this wheezy, old cabbage..." he answered with some grimace, trying to perk himself up.

"So do you know what's going on or are you going to keep it to yourself? Is it bad?" he asked in a whisper, hoping not to stir trouble with the youngsters.

"Yes, but you wouldn't believe me. You'll just have to wait and hope you get lucky. That's how most of us stay this luck, it's all just pure-luck," the grandfather answered with a sigh, turning away slightly from his grandson in defeat.

"Does it have to do with the "visitors" at least, are they real or just gossip?" he pressed further onto his grandfather.

"… I'm getting tired, ask me later once I wake up from my afternoon nap," the grandfather ended, almost sounding like a plea than a request.

It seemed his grandfather had already fallen into a dead slumber before he could retort in persistence. He knew he wasn't going to divine any other information. He groaned in irritation but respectfully complied with his elder's wishes. He would just enjoy the autumn weather, listen to the other children play in the soil, perhaps enjoy the sun with some nourishment. Then these "visitors" might conclude their unimaginable business that they may have with his family. His train of thought, however, was abruptly interrupted by the disappearance of the giggling children. It had become eerily silent suddenly without warning, and the entire family seemed to cease their banter. He turned to both sides but saw nothing. Then he heard footsteps bellowing like a giant as the ground shook in slow intervals. His body felt cold and lifeless, and so he turned back to his grandfather.

"Did you hear that? Wake up, I think something is here but… I don't see anything," he whisper, desperate to alert him and receive an answer quickly.

There was no reply, intentionally oblivious and sleep or not, and so moved onto the children that began to nestle together in fear. Weakly, he attempted to reassure his siblings with a kind smile.

"Don't worry, they wouldn't be allowed in the farm without a reason, they won't hurt any of you."

"Oh, what about those two?" spoke a voice from behind.

A colossus-sized shadow approached, looming over his sleeping grandfather and himself. He was racked with suspicious fear, leaving him speechless as he tried to make sense of the impending gloom.

"Yeah, I can see us using these two. Can you grab the older-looking one?" spoke another voice.

Before he could react or even speak out, he felt the presence of this visitor. He saw the horrifying expression over his siblings' faces, what it must have meant. He heard a snap, and his head filled with a snaring, throbbing ache like a bone had splintered in half in a clean, separating break. Then everything went dark.

#

Startled, he awoke to a blinding light, dazed and confused as he looked around the room with a groggy stare. His sight blurred like a palette of watercolors, and the voices seemed to sound distant and strange like a faint murmur. From the chorus of sounds, he made out one of the voices clearly, bit by bit, and he looked across the room to see his grandfather. It seemed some unknown, looming figure was confronting him. He tried to make out what they were saying, but his grandfather sounded muffled and gagged. Finally, he noticed the wet, serrated knife in the giant's hand.

"Wh-what's going on, what are you doing to him?! Grandpa, are you alright?!" he yelled, but there was no reply as the giants continued their work.

"I think it's done, promise you won't laugh at it, Diana?" spoke one of his kidnappers as it brandished the knife, wiping the blade with a towel.

"Don't worry, give yourself a bit more credit," answered another voice behind her, but he couldn't see who or what.

"Okay…" she turned his grandfather over and displayed his remains to the group, "what do you think?"

He was instantly horrified beyond comprehension, never seeing such brutal cruelty on a living being without provocation. He could barely contain himself, fighting the urge to empty the contents of his stomach out onto the floor. His grandfather was unrecognizable as his entire face scarred with lacerations. Some incisions left gaping gashes in his head. There were parts of his skin peeled and pieces obliterated, leaving a deformed assemblage. Beneath the Cheshire smile, he could hear the resigned but long-suffering voice spill out, looking at his grandson with sorrow:

"I-m s-o-r-r-y . . . f-o-r-g-i-v-e . . . m- e . . ."

"Wha-what, wh-wh-why is this happening!?!" he shouted, accusingly looking at their tormentors, "YOU SAVAGES, what ar-"

"Honestly, I think it's cute but if you want some help, you can watch me cut this one up," she said, oblivious to his cries.

He was left speechless; he couldn't understand how this could be happening to them or why they were so discarded by the two huddled behind him. It was only then he realized that he was the next victim. Before he could protest or defend himself, he felt the cold steel pierce his head. There was an overwhelming shot of agony rip through him until he felt the knife tear and wiggle through his nerves, severing any sensation for a brief time. The executioner continued to saw through the rim of his skull. At the same time, they both conversed casually, falling on his deaf ears:

"Obviously, you'll need to make an opening and scoop up the insides...."

He could feel his chrome latched off, his brain matter exposed like to a surgeon, he began to twitch and spaz in place. Then he felt the knife continue its surgery, digging into the backside of his skull.

"But you could also cut the back, it makes emptying out the body easier. It's easier to place the candle too."

"c-c-c-c-an-d-d-d-le?"

"O-h g-o-d . . . h-e-l-p u-s. . ."

"Wh-wh-wh-wh-a-a-a-a-t . . . i-s . . . a . . . c-a-n-d-"

But before he could think futilely further, she turned his head. He faced his captors, reeling in disgust by their hideous, enormous visage. It was as if she were riddled with strange sores, misshaped appendages with colored orbs, which he guessed were its eyes. And porcelain-like teeth, grinning and chattering from the corners of their mouths. Despite his screams, pleading, protesting, or his threats to get his well-deserved revenge upon these two butchers, she kept digging into his flesh. She cut shapes around his face, pulling out chucks that jump-started the nerve endings to pain once more. He began crying like a lost banshee out to sea, searching for remorse and pity towards his withering husk. He found only a short reprieve as she placed the dagger on the table with a satisfied smile, proud of her hacking handiwork as the other looked onward with awe:

"Oh wow," she replied, "you made a little cat, that's so adorable. It's too bad we don't have any matching ears like a headband to go with it."

"Ah, that's the trick," she chuckled, taking the dagger in hand again, "You use the cut-out eyes for the ears. I just need to cut some more holes near the top of the head."

"Pl-pl-pleeeeea-se, s-t-o-p . . ."

But she continued to pay no attention to him, turning a blind eye to his weeping complexion or listening to his moaning wails. She slid the knife down on top of his head, removing small sections in boxed shapes. Then she slabbed the leftover piece of his remains into the carved slots like some twisted ornaments oozing from the sides.

"M-y g-o-d . . . w-h-a-t a-r-e y-o-u d-o-i-n-g t-o m-y b-o-y . . ." the grandfather lamented, unable to do anything to prevent the massacre.

"There, NOW we have a cat but minus the tail, still working on that part out," she said, with some short-lived triumph as she wanted that tail badly.

"Heh, don't worry, we still have some time before Halloween," the other consoled, "should we test them out and see how they look?"

"Sounds good, I'll grab the lighter," she answered, leaving her side and out of sight.

"No . . . n-o-n-o-n-o-n-o-n-o-n-o-n-o-n-o-n-o-n-o-n-o!" the grandfather screamed, trying great lengths to escape and move but to no prevail.

His grandson could only hear his grandfather start to sob and pray for release, filling him with more infallible despair. Their captors returned, holding strange objects in their hands. His initial captor, the one called "Diana" that sliced opened his body, had a slender, shiny rod with a black gap running down, accompanied by a red handle. She slid a finger between the loop. Her accomplice, the one called "Jocelyn," appeared behind and carried two fat bundles with a waxy complexion and pale-brown coloring, smelling like cinnamon. But he couldn't tell any further as she hopped over, moving behind the two of them, the grandson and the grandfather.

"You're right, it is easier to put the candles inside once you open the backside," she said, tearing their skulls back out and feeling some placed directly into their ripped cavity.

He could feel the weight against his neck, the shape brushed up on his inner flesh, the pressure indenting and mashing his lifeblood. However, it wasn't as painful as before; the wave had grown null over his body. But, judging from his grandfather's continuous cries, he felt this was when the beasts would strike down on their unwilling, unknowing prey again.

"Okay, let's get this Halloween party started!" Diana laughed, snapping the trigger of her device.

Suddenly, a light struck the end of the rod like lighting in a storm, blinding his sight, and once returned, greeted by a mysterious yet wondrous orb. He had never witnessed such a thing. It was a small, tiny orb with a living, orange-yellow aura that seemed to breathe around it. The light from the flashing orb felt warm like the rays of the sun during midday, and it made him tingle tenderly with its soothing spark. It almost erased all the suffering. Still, he noticed his grandfather flinching away, and as the creature drew closer and closer, he felt the trance lift slowly. The orb was inches away from his face. He felt his skin blister and crack like ice and made him squirm and tense up. His bliss had turned to anxious fright as she pushed the orb further. What was this creature planning to do with it, he thought?

"Let's see that handsome smile glow," it said, slipping the rod past his torn hole and light the wick of the candle.

It didn't take very long; the candle was ablaze soon. It grew into a fierce inferno. The flames licked at the inner walls of his mind, roasting what little remained inside of the body. This sensation was all new to him, burning away at his sanity as it continued to roar amidst his screams. It felt as if his entire being knew only of suffering, no longer transfixed by the previous encounters, only slowly burning out at the center of his nerves. His brain could only feel the raging fire.

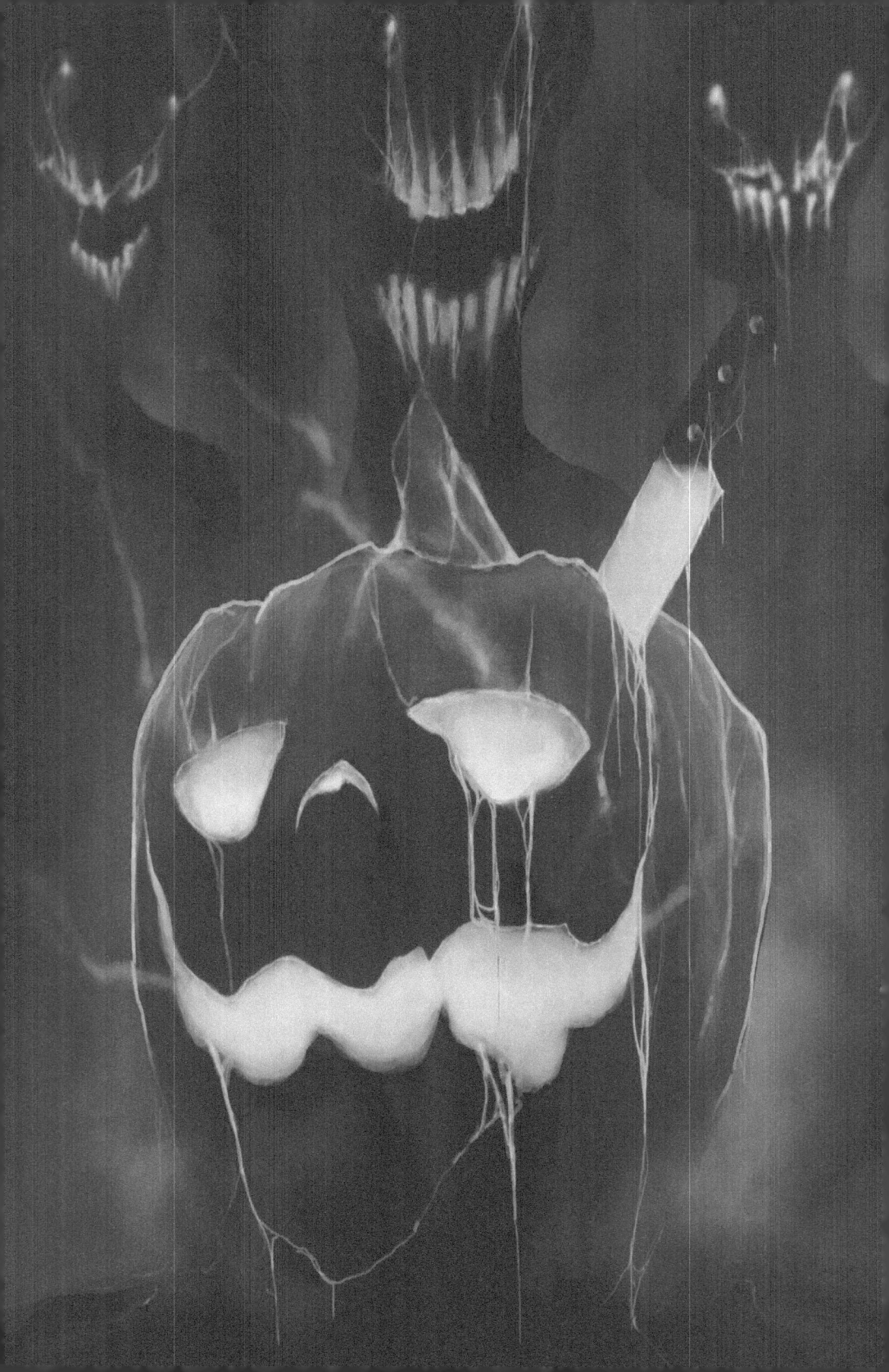

He couldn't speak other than his deafening shrieks; he couldn't hear his grandfather as he too began to howl like a wounded animal. Nor could he see clearly within the near-blinding torment. The flames continued their onslaught, scorching at their insides, crackling as his pieces only fed the heat.

"Hey Mom, can you turn off the lights?" Jocelyn cried out, turning behind her as the other looked onward with such delight.

"Sure thing sweetie," called out a disembodied voice, followed by a flurry of shuffling steps and a clicking sound like a beetle to a reed.

Instantly, the room became shrouded with faint darkness, with the flames licking at his skeletal grin and casting some small light ahead of him. In a matter of seconds, ghoulish faces surrounded the duo in the dim, flickering light. These creatures forced him to watch, drawing closer with their own disfigured features leering overhead, unable to tear himself from their gaze. With their prying, bugged eyes and jeering smiles, this family of homicidal lunatics began to snicker, giggle, and laugh at his dismay and gruesome fate. The shadows melted over their expressions in a menacing hysteria that felt like he lost himself in a fever dream. All the while, his burning skull began to broil his body. It forced him to bear a grin despite his misery. His wails flooded and eclipsed by their maddening laughter.

One of the creatures, riddled with wrinkles and folds of skin, held another strange device in her boney, malformed hands, and he dreaded the worse. She moved it to his face, and a flash of light shocked his eyes and repeated this process several times over. The creature flipped the device over and became giddity, the other creatures huddling closer together as if they were melding into one, looking over the strange device and its platform. The older creature flipped the machine again, revealing a captured image, and he could barely see. Still, it seemed to be a mirror to his destruction. From what he could tell, they seemed to be achieving these images of his grandfather and himself, mounting their carved, abused mutilations like trophies over the hearth.

"Great job, sweetie. You too, Jocelyn, very classical," congratulated the older creature, directing her attention to the two, sliding the strange image-capturing device somewhere behind her.

"Let's blow out the candle and put them outside for now, the other neighbors are putting their jack-o-lanterns out," suggested Jocelyn, grabbing his grandfather by the bottom.

"Sure, why not?" replied Diana, snuffing out the wick with her foul breath against his frail, orange nose.

And just like that, the pain had nearly vanished, and he left an uneasy relief once more, bewildered at this sudden peace. They carried the duo off, and he could barely witness his surroundings as it changed swiftly in sight. He couldn't even speak to his gibbering grandfather. He managed to talk, at last, only slightly subdued by the persistent throbbing against the skull, clouding his speech partially:

"Wh-wh-where a-a-a-re the-the-the-e-e-ey ta-a-a-aking u-s?"

". . . to h-e-l-l . . ." groaned his grandfather, and the two felt a sudden chill in the air as they pass through a wooden archway with metal fittings and an apparent lock.

It was far darker outside than it was inside their home. He could hear the wind and the insects chirping as it did back at the farm. The evening breeze, however, felt more harsh and rigid in comparison, biting at their skin and clawing away at their flesh. It seemed only to get colder and colder with the coming winter air freezing their blood, causing them to shiver and tremble against the bleak, icy atmosphere enclosed around them. There was no end to their plight, the wind whipping at them from all sides without protection. First, their blood was boiling, but now, it became like a frozen river. The shift to these extreme temperatures caused their minds to fog, their thoughts becoming hazy as they struggled to stay conscious amidst the cold, miserable agony. And there they remained, left and abandoned on the concrete steps, watching those torturers flee the scene of the crime.

"Shouldn't we light them up again," asked Jocelyn, huddling close to her as the wind picked up shortly.

"Naw, they'll last longer and I don't want to stay out longer, this wind is killing me," complained Diana, hugging Joceyln to her bosom.

As they left, the grandson could see the outline of the neighboring houses faintly; dots of lights littered the area. As he looked onward, he started to hear the low weeping and wailing vertebrate the world. The echoes of his fallen brethren fell victim to their own kidnapping as he listened and watched with surreal, unearthly dismay. More and more of their ripped, grotesque faces flare with a fiery glow, stretched out into imprisoned rows without any release as the madmen left them in the cold.

What could be worse, death by fire or by cold? The answer was both in an everlasting state.

He wouldn't have to fear the cold or the fire anymore as he heard snickering coming from the shadows, then he felt grimy hands grip around his body as they pulled away from the stoop. He could only watch as his grandfather disappeared from sight, being carried off in a stampede while only hearing his voice trail off:

"It... will... be... quick... ... farewell... my... precious... boy...."

"What about the other pumpkin?"

"Nah, it's too nasty, better to leave it...."

He didn't have the strength, courage, or willpower to contest whatever was going to happen next. A part of him felt only guilt that he left his grandfather with so much remorse and a trickle of tranquility that shamed him. Nevertheless, he was relieved, knowing he wasn't condemned to his grandfather's fate. But what WOULD they do to him?

They were soon speeding at great length, hosted onto a strange vehicle, almost similar to the tractor accustomed to on the farm but less bulky and slender. It wasn't long before he heard the disembodied voices laugh and plot away:

"Ready?"

"Yeah, HAPPY HALLOWEEN!"

Immediately, he launched into the air, and time seemed to crawl as he descended towards the ground gradually. He could see from a side glimpse; the vehicle was swerving uncontrollably. It disappeared into the night, as did the hyena-like laughter. His attention directed back at the approaching ground, pitch-black tar that seemed to open up into an abyss. Soon, he knew, the impact would shatter his hollowed head, and it would finally end at last. He patiently welcomed the blow, closing his eyes and wondering what would be next for him. His final thoughts were this:

"I hope the others will stay safe…."

He felt a sudden stop, a sharp pain, and then nothing. It was finally over, with his remains splattered across the road.

END OF THE NIGHT

October 30th

The Creature

It was nightfall, the day before Halloween. Beyond the boardwalk, along the shore, the lake laid bare except for a sole individual. The sand felt cold and clammy, rough clumps between his toes as he scrunched his feet and looked outward to the sea. Its waters had extended its reach by the waning moon, reflecting amongst the stars onto the dark blue surface, resembling a mural of exquisite charcoal and gemstone whites. These waves would quietly breach the shoreline, then recede back into the ocean with a rumbling echo. Despite the serenity and lovely view, it bore no comfort to him.

The salty air stung his eyes as they began to water and swell up. He stared defiantly into that vast horizon and cursed under his breath. He peered back onto his phone's screen, lighting up his face and revealing the dark, sullen rings underneath his eyes from sleep deprivation. He gritted his teeth sharply as he rang his fingers across the screen, cascading a gallery of photos of Jocelyn over the social network. These particular photos had a short, petite lady accompanying her in various poses at the local farm like a sequential slideshow, ending up at their house on a table, carving two pumpkins joyously. All of which had the two brimming with a loving embrace and carefree smile. It had only been a few weeks, and she had moved onward, seemingly forgotten him altogether. She was happy while he had only gotten worse without her...

He stood there, staring at the short, petite whore, then he bellowed out a scream that rang out across the lake like a dying animal. With a tremendous amount of strength, appearing from the deepest part of his unhinged psyche, he flung his phone out into the ocean without a second thought. It flew further than one would've expected, like some Olympian shot-put, and landed deep into the black waters. For a moment, he froze in that position, staring out into the ocean as if slowly processing what he just did. He looked at his empty hand, then back at sea. His face winced into a contorted expression as he began to realize he had thrown his phone into the ocean. Taking a few steps back, he ran his fingers through his hair as he started to spaz and curse loudly:

"shit fuck shit... FUCK! Now I have to pay for a new phone, gawdfuckingdammit!!!"

After his mad dance had settled down, he looked back at the ocean and felt it had gotten colder than before. He took a few steps forward and then stopped, falling onto his knees, and began to sob into the night. He couldn't understand why he had come out here or what good it would do him. The tears felt like ice running down his cheeks, a mixture of defeat and depressing isolation as if on a stranded island. He sank further into the brittle cold sand, it digging into the skin of his thighs and legs as he continued to kneel down. The wind whipped into a short frenzy, causing the chilling air to rip into his watery eyes even more. He gritted his teeth, still sobbing but growled underneath his bated breath. His hands flung upward to his face, shielding his eyes beneath cupped palms as the whirlwind of sand and saltwater twirled around him. He would continue to sob for some time, cursing the world and Jocy with it. However, a part of him wanted the world to comfort him and give him something to hold onto now. It all just seemed to fade away, the sound of his surroundings becoming meek like a hermit-crab. It took some effort to stir him from his trance until a gentle voice spoke to him:

"Excuse me, sir? I'm sorry but are you alright?"

He looked up, and staring down at him was a pair of the most dazzling clear-green eyes on the most enchanting woman he had ever seen. In the darkness of the night, her eyes shown like gemstones that seemed both piercing yet pleasantly calm. His eyes adjusted, and he could see her flawless skin was a dark shade of olive-brown tan, presumably from basking in the sun, and thus, gave the figure a warm, comforting aura. Likewise, she seemed to have a slender jawline yet defined chin, a Romanesque nose gracing the center of her face. The most profound trait to this woman was perhaps her flowing jet-black hair that draped past her shoulders like a mane of a mare; it was still wet with saltwater, and bits of seaweed was in the locks of her hair. It was strange, but he noticed her ears were slightly crooked and pointed, partially hidden by her hair, but he felt they were horse-like as well. At that moment, her voice broke the trance he was spell struck by:

"Sir, did you hear me? Is something wrong, do you need help?" she replied, more concerned than before. She reached out her hand, partially looming over him.

"OH... yes, I'm sorry. I'm just surprised anyone was here... at this late hour..." the man partially lied, primarily to himself for staring so awkwardly at her.

He complied with her offer, slipping his fingers into her awaiting grasp. As he got up to his feet, he tried to swat away the tears from his eyes. During that transition, he leaned closer and smelled a wonderful aroma of shea-butter and shaved coconut coming off of her body that made him slightly weak in the knees. He took a step back and found the rest of her as impressive.

She was roughly small in her height with a trim build like a seasoned swimmer. She was undoubtedly trained with her toned muscles and wearing a long, black spandex swim-leotard. Her arms, legs, and abdomen were twitching with sharp definition and still glistening with water droplets like morning dew. At her feet, an ancient-looking duffle bag laid open. In the crook of her arm was the towel. However, what threw him off was her feet were buried into the sand, past her ankles. He wondered how she kept her balance, if that was comfortable, or if she was doing that on purpose; he couldn't see any part of his feet. He quickly recovered, telling himself it was trivial.

She retrieved the towel wrapped around her arm and started wringing off her matted hair, still addressing him:

"I completely understand, it's a surprise for me that anyone is on the lake this late too," she said shortly, an eye peeking out from the towel, "so why ARE you here?"

He blushed a bit, the redness in his cheeks becoming like ripe tomatoes, but he hoped she couldn't see him clearly with the towel; he should've seen that question coming. He tussled a lock of his hair past his forehead, fidgeting to find a proper retort but thus mistakenly returning back to the thought of Jocelyn again as a result:

"I'd go to this lake with my... my ex-girlfriend... it use to feel great... coming down here, no matter the time or reason... closest thing to a day at the beach, I guess."

"Oh, I'm sorry, did you want to be alone or would you like someone to talk about it?"

"Well I can't just ask you to leave, you were here first," he said, debating the options himself, "and I think talking about it would help a little. Besides, I shouldn't be alone this late."

"Alright then," she moved to her side and sat down on the sand, then motioned him to follow suit with a pat to the ground, "let's get started."

He smiled faintly and did so, crouching down and sitting next to her. As he did, she swung her towel over his shoulders unexpectedly and quick, which shocked him, but she had responded back:

"I'm fine, I don't need it so don't feel like you need to be chivalrous with me, you need it more."

He would've rejected the offer politely, but he noticed the towel wasn't wet or even damp but rather fluffy and warm, oddly dry against his skin. Gripping the towel closer to his shoulders, he glanced at the lady's endowed chest; it was still glistening with water against the fabric. He would've continued to leer at them if she hadn't interrupted his train of fantasizing thought:

"Don't worry, I know I'm still wet but after years of swimming, you get use to the cold too," she answered, thinking he was concern about her health, misjudging his stare. Nervously, as a teenage schoolgirl, he chuckled and pulled his hair back behind another ear again. The swimmer, wrapping her arms around her legs close to her chest, rested her chin between her knees. She looked onward with an eager expression on her face:

"I'm all ears now, talk whatever you feel like talking and I'll listen," she promised him, tenderly like a lover.

Flustered, he exhaled a breath. He loosened the tension in his muscles and began speaking his mind at last. And so, they sat in that spot, facing the shoreline, talking about his breakup with his previous girlfriend, taking the time to emphasize his newfound availability to a relationship now. The stranger simply nodded respectfully, hanging onto every word intently with undivided attention. He continued to explain his mixed anguish and jealously at how quickly her girlfriend had moved on without him… especially going out with the same-sex, taking it as a personal offense for being inadequate or being strung along for a ride. At the same time, however, he confessed he didn't want to feel that he seemed like a misogynist or force social expectations on anyone in this day and age. It seemed like he argued for hours, but he was never interrupted, nor did she show any signs of boredom until he was done and caught up with the present at last. When all was said and done, the stranger finally gave her response:

"It's never easy being rejected, but you shouldn't blame yourself completely. It sounds like she didn't realize her attraction until it happened, she discovered who she was and now the two of you can be who you were meant to be."

"I guess… you could look at it that way," he agreed, reluctantly, looking over to the side. However, he quickly withdrew his gaze when he felt his hand touched by her and looked back at the strange woman. He found her emerald eyes locked onto him like lighthouses guiding sailors to safety; it seemed warm and gentle yet invasive.

"I know you may be in pain but I promise you that someone will be there to take away that pain soon," she vowed, her fingers tenderly wrapped around his open palm.

"Um… th-thank you," he stammered, not knowing how to react to her. She was forward with mixed signals, yet she seemed to honestly care from out of the blue.

"I know, I'm moving a bit fast and presumption, my friends warned me I'd scare away the good ones…."

"Oh well, I wouldn't say that," he retorted, only to realize that she may have been trying to flirt with him more.

"Hey, how about we go for a swim?"

"Wait, wha-"

But she had already pulled him up from the spot and leading onward towards the shore. They were almost halfway, he couldn't believe how strong she was, and she seemed so adamant about the idea that it seemed wrong to say no. Despite that, however, he managed an excuse:

"Now? I don't have any swim trucks with me. Why not another time, like, during the day?"

"That's easy, just take off your clothes," she interjected, not looking back at him in a serene yet severe tone.

"It's a bit cold for me," he tried again, meekly and ashamed of himself for sounding like a whining brat to his mother.

"Well," she stopped short, their feet in the saltwater, and turned to face him, "I guess I'll have to stay close by...."

She said this with such an elusive smile. It made the gentleman nearly faint and skip a beat. Slowly, she receded back into the ocean, her eyes staring back at his without looking behind herself as if she were a native to the waters. The moonlight cascaded across and shined brilliantly like a pearl against satin with the reflection of the near-still water. Her eyes seemed to glow supernaturally alongside the moon, luring him into a trance as her beauty began to radiate into a glow. Against his better judgment, he began to disrobe and cast the articles to the side, diving into the sand and disappearing from his sight and memory. It wasn't long before he was down to only his boxers, staring at the enchanting siren. A few steps closer, and he felt the harsh coldness again.

His muscles reacted, taking a few steps back and felt his skin crawl, the hairs standing on ends across his torso. He looked at the slow-reaching waves, then back at the lady, who was giggling and nearly waist-deep.

"It's a bit colder than I imagined," he laughed, trying to be convincing and perhaps persuade her to leave instead.

"It'll get warmer once you're in, especially if you hold onto me close," she remarked, stroking her wet hair and part some strands from her eyes.

"Ar-are you sure it's safe?" he asked, trying to steel himself and demolish any anxiety left in him as he moves in further.

"There's always a risk for any reward...." she cooed, kneeling down, so only her neck and head were exposed. Shortly after, an arm emerged from the dark waters and in her hand, dangling from her fingertips, her unlatched bikini-top, which she twirled like a fan before flinging it away so nonchalantly.

The loss of his cellphone to the ocean, the loss of his previous girlfriend: they seemed like a distant thought. The icy water lost all effect on him; it was no longer an obstacle as he made his way through the dark pool. He had a significant journey wading through, only to find she had disappeared from view. His eyes darted across to the sides, then turning around to re-discover his treasured prize, but he noticed that they were further out than he had anticipated. Looking down, he saw that he was in deep, the water sloshing against the chest mid-level, and he would've been in more profound, up to his neck, if he hadn't kept balance and taken a step back on the slimy sand beneath him.

Suddenly, the water exploded behind him, and he felt the frigid embrace wrapped around his shoulders. He started to frail and fling his arms as he screamed in a short high-pitch, only drowned by a peal of laughter erupted in his ears.

"I'm sorry, I couldn't help myself. You're too cute when you're scared," she apologized, stroking his shoulder blades before dropping to his lower back.

He would've protested against such a claim, emphasizing the fact that she threw him off-guard and blind-sided him completely; anyone would've been 'scared' by her attack. But he realized she was still naked, her bare breasts pressed against his back, he could feel her erect nipples poke his skin, and he felt so warm again. He was almost afraid to turn around and face her; he was worried he'd scare her off as if she were a timid creature. As he turned, she kept her arms loosely around his waist, her fingers sinking into the flesh of his exposed back. He looked down and saw a large amount of cleavage smooched against his abs as she held onto him. She looked up, smiling sweet and innocently before she rested her head against his chest, closing her eyes and listening to his quicken heartbeat. Compelled, he drifted his arms and placed them gingerly on her in an embrace, stroking her long hair tenderly. He never felt this way with another girl before, which made him think and blurt out:

"Why me?"

"I like..." she began, almost in a slumbering stupor, "to play... with my food...."

"Wait, what?"

He looked down. That's when he noticed their reflection in the quiet tide, shown in the pale moonlight like a mirror. At first, he thought it was a trick of the light or distortion in the waves or a piece of drifting seaweed. But the more he stared, the more apparent it became that it was authentic. Her reflection appeared to be dark, a mess of hair tangled in clumps everywhere. As he stared deeper, he could make out the face, expecting to see her lovely visage. Instead, he found a more equine shape crooked and loomed over her body like a scythe. Its maw wrapped around its face, but he could see a thin boney ridge. Its eyes were sickly-white like orbs of dim light from the ends of a watering hole or a well, rings sunken into the skull. Down the ridge of its skeletal bridge, its maw was outstretched with rows of elongated teeth, broken and sharpen but broad like broken planks of wood from a dying sea-faring vessel. The mouth was open wide as if the hinges of its jaw were dislocated, similar to snakes when they swallowed their prey whole. Its mouth was gaping, overshadowing its head as if preparing to rip his skull off, a diseased-green tongue slithering around his neck like a noose.

Slowly, he released his hold on her, dropping his arms to the side, and allowed his hands to drift like oars to a boat. He tried to avoid arousing her, looking past his shoulders casually, determining how far they were out to sea. It made him shiver as he noticed the growing distance from the land. They were further out to sea than he had imagined. He felt around his feet, paddling to stay afloat and, as he couldn't grasp the sandy floor anymore, knew they were in deep. She hadn't let go of him, her nails digging into his skin like hooks; she had become adhesive onto him. He tried to coerce his way from her clutches, unable to hide his nervous chuckle, which broke the tension like a broken bottle:

"Not to be a drag but don't you think we should head back?"

"Yeah, you're right... I should go home now...."

The two shot down into the watery void, plunging in cold darkness without warning like a heavy anchor released from its ship

He felt his lungs burst as the air escaped his mouth into a stream of bubbles, trailing to the surface as he continued to dive deeper. There was no use for him to scream, and even with his arms free, he couldn't pull himself quick or strong enough to break free from her grasp. A rush of water trickled fast down his throat, his tears mixing with the ocean, burning his eyes as the pressure began to push against him from all sides. The edges of reason blurred, and fear lurched deep into his stomach. He was faced with immediate death as the girl began to dissolve in seafoam and show the ghastly form he had seen on the water's surface before. Her head thrashed about and convulsed over his face as she unlatched her jaws and prepared herself to consume him. Her wide gaping mouth, littered with rows of crooked serrated teeth, left him breathless and cold than ever before. Her pitiless eyes stared at him hungrily, his soul seemingly sucked out by her dead gaze and a sliver of disgust as his arms brushed against its rotten, water-clogged skin, tangled by its black mane.

He didn't have any other choice, however, and so he fought quickly in response to his life, desperately clawed at the water and the creature, holding her mouth open like a crocodile. He tried to shoot to the surface, his lungs swamped with slimy liquid as he convulsed uncontrollably. He thought it would simply shut the jaws on him, the creature seemed stronger than him, but she began to wheel back and twitch for an odd reason. He stopped short and then put his hands on her throat, trying to choke it when he noticed a glimmer around his finger like a torch. As he pressed his hand further, he saw it was the silver ring he had left on his right hand, and it started to react to the creature's body. It flashed and appeared to be a flaming lime-green orb at the tip of the ring, burning across the flesh and ripping shreds. The remains that came off became like turf and a soft mass like jellyfish, floating and dissipating quickly.

The creature began to scream into jets of bubbles, the sound echoing in the darkness as she felt her throat flare and burn like St. Elmo's fire. Immediately, she released him, and he began to frantically. The pain had subsided, but she was burning with intense hatred towards her prey. She was consumed by wrath with a well-spring of power than she had possessed ever before. She began to chase after him, closing after him, left without much strength to stay below too long. He felt his arms go numb and weightless as he stroked upward while his legs began to dangle and twist helplessly like a fish on a hook. He knew she'd be on him soon, the head-start had little effect, but his last thoughts were the silver. He realized and knew that he still had one last attempt at life that could work, based on what he observed with the creature. She hadn't noticed before that he was wearing a silver cross…

He ripped the necklace from his neck. She speeded up towards the surface faster, howling in pain and stretching her mouth, preparing to tear him apart in her anger and hunger like a mad shark. He wrapped the chain around his clenched fist, and as she was only a few inches away from his torso, he launched his arm straight into her gullet. He felt his fist puncture something soft like the end of her throat and quickly retracted his arm out before she could react further. She doubled back and stared viciously at him, but not before noticing he was without his silver cross. Her neck twisted, started to shrink, and close up, burning away at her insides as the silver began to melt her flesh. She began to rend her webbed-claws at her throat, but she could feel her life slip away, and for the first time, she began to experience what it was like to drown. Descending slowly to the depths, she stared back as her prey managed to escape to the surface and flee the ocean in haste. She stretched out her hand, which started to pulse and bloat into bubbles of flesh, breaking into foam once more. It wouldn't be long; she didn't have the energy left to fight against her nature and weakness. That man would live while she'd be dead and fabricated as a distant nightmare. The thought of losing her family, losing sight of her sisters as the image of them flashed in her mind, gave away to unrelenting sorrow. She lost hold of any consciousness and drifted into the vast, menacing sea, and the last thing she could remember before she slipped away was the pain and emptiness.

Her last and only thought was:

"Fucking men... can't live with them... and without them... damnit..."

END OF THE NIGHT

October 31st

The End

The author will finish your story,
this being the final enclave.
Tread carefully through the allegory,
avoid his dug grave.

He stared into the card, unable to process the bizarre information that was delivered to him. Slowly, he turned the card over to the other side to see any other messages written on like a serial number. It was smooth and blank, the gloss shining like polished metal. Flipping the card back to its front, efforts were re-doubled to decipher the near-poetic code, rebounding on his creeping insecurity. At a certain level, he could understand that it was a promotion of his timely death. However, he had trouble understanding the "author," which must be some sort of metaphor. But it seemed hauntingly odd to him:

"Hey Tom, you make these cards yourself or what?" asked Nemo.

"Naw, and I don't need to be a psychic to know what you'll ask next," Tom answered, "so I'll tell you what I told the others, I don't know how that thing makes these predictions but they do seem to be weirdly specific...."

He looked back at the machine-booth, wondering if there was a trick to it. Around the machine, he inspected the exterior, kneeling down and feeling around the walls, eyeing for any slots or hinges that could reveal a compartment. These predictions WERE too specific, almost sophisticated, randomly selected, or printed out by some pre-recorded template. He needed to find the logical explanation for all of this. He found none; he didn't even find the electrical cord. This was not something that he could condone. He couldn't handle any more otherworldly bullshit like the night before. If it was supernatural in nature, then he felt that he wouldn't be lucky twice.

Reaching into his pocket, he found another quarter and slipped it into the coin slot again. The quarter, however, did not go through as if it was blocked by something. The booth started back up despite the apparent hindrance, which startled Nemo, looking up at the fortune-teller's expression. It glowed and shimmered across its visage, the hands glazed over the crystal ball as it faded in and out with a misty effect. Nemo stood up, confused and concerned, but he rationalized that it may have been a fluke like those breaks in the soda machine where you get a free can by mistake. All the same, he awaited with anxiety, wondering what was going to happen next. The booth started to seem like the jaws of that monster, ready to swallow his head whole and his immediate thought of the creature. The fortune-teller stopped abruptly, slowly raised her head with a clicking sound, and stared directly into Nemo's eyes. It raised an eyebrow and gave a verbal reply in a sarcastic tone with a heavy accent:

"Sorry kid, I don't do re-dos or give refunds…."

Nemo staggered backward. He whirled around to face Tommy still behind the counter of the tavern. He had already put his hands up in defense, shaking his head without any hint of jest. He whipped back at the booth, but it had grown silent and dark, the fortune-teller returning to a lifeless slumber. It merely stood there like some gravestone, growing colder and merciless, distant from the rest of the world. But Nemo didn't know which was worse, the silence or the answer.

"That's new, I didn't think she could talk…." Tom replied, "But she's got a charm, people are going around talking about her and when the word hits, BOOM! I'll be back in business again."

With that, he gathered his things and grabbed his coat from the peg off the wall. He waved to Tom, who nodded his head in reply, and he left the tavern at the late hour. As he closed the door, he glanced at the streets and found it deserted, imagining that everyone had retired from their Halloween night. All with their loved ones, safe in their homes and in a warm embrace. All except him…

With a click of his tongue, sucking through his teeth, he stormed off while wishing to himself that he get a chance to take it all back. If only he could get his ex-girlfriend back... if only he visited the fortune-teller days before... maybe, he would've gotten some insight on that instead...

Cursing under his breath, he crossed the street to the other side and made her way to his house. He popped his coat collar and zipped up, trying to shield himself from the sudden chill in the air as the wind cut his face like icicle shards. His boots clipped away at the concrete pavement like metal horse-shoes onto hooves. The noise carried with the gust of wind as he heard the presiding rustle of leaves join the chorus. He tried to block it out; it annoyed him for some reason until he noticed the streetlamps began to flicker above. Looking up, it continued to flash faster and faster, which made him hesitate and turn front and back. All of the lights were shuttering violently. And like a bolt of lightning, all of the bulbs shattered and filled with darkness, giving an instant shrill. Then it grew silent. It was eerily quiet that it became unnerving for him; he felt defenseless and unseen by the rest of the world.

Slowly, he saw the shadows lengthen and grow, which may not have been a surprise, but it seemed more adamant and animated than average. He could sense there was an unnatural presence, and the longer he stared into the void, it became more apparent. The darkness seemed to creep from the path he had crossed from the bar, tendrils that swept the ground and air that sucked everything in its body. More and more, all seemed to break away into nothingness. Even the stars above seemed to be eclipsed and blotted out by an outstretched hand. It grew darker and darker, speeding up towards him at a gradual transition. There was Nothing left in its grasp. All sight and sound had seemingly been erased from existence by complete shadow. He backed away slowly, unable to comprehended or react appropriately to this new threat.

From the back of his neck, he could feel his hairs stand up as some of the tendrils wrapped around a heel. The moment he felt those shadows brush against him, he sensed a wave of... what he imagined evaporation might be like... but dark as if he were receding into a vacuum of space. A threshold of fear had been reached within him, one that he recalled from before, and he knew what must be there. Although far from being an expert, he had recognized that familiar monstrous feeling creeps up at him.

It was like Nemo was a rabbit ensnared onto an iron-sprung trap and caught by the vicious wolf. He started to tremble at last, cold sweat beading down his face, afraid to move as the shadows crept closer. It seemed to be waiting on his subsequent reaction, jeering him on to make a move to start the chase and hunt. But he couldn't die, he thought, not after all he was put through before.

He took another step back, then retreated but shortly stopped as he saw the other side was closed off by the entrenching shadow, swallowing any means of escape as well as the world entirely. It almost seemed as the ground around him was breaking away into a void, leaving him stranded in an ever-shrinking island. He looked around, all the sides appeared to follow the same fate, and no one seemed to notice. It was as if they were being removed from the universe without so much as a whimper. The buildings from the town seemed to collapse and faded into blackness as they consumed more and more space. He looked behind him, and he saw the gate unlatched, leading to the graveyard. He was left unable to question it; the cemetery seemed a safe haven as it was left untouched by this nothingness. Without any alternative, he raced through the gate, not noticing it close behind and lock as he darted further into the misty gale. He didn't dare look back, not until he found a way out…

#

Without thinking, Nemo continued to run without looking behind him. He wouldn't bear the thought of the darkness chasing him. His surroundings faded from his sight, scrambling to find footing in the damp, course earth. It didn't even cross his mind as he raced around the grave-markers, climbing over burial mounds, and hid beneath the shadows from the columns of a mausoleum. However, he didn't stop there and continued to run like a mouse trapped within a maze, with all possible exits seemingly closed off. For a while, he sprinted through the deathly plain until it hurt his lungs to breathe, and his sides began to split apart. It felt like his legs would give out and fall off, choosing to finally rest behind one of the grave-markers. Under cover of darkness, the harvest moon hidden behind dense clouds, he felt somewhat hidden from the unsuspecting world and, thus, from the end of the world.

That shred of hope fell short when he saw from the corner of his eyes, followed by the creeping shadows that wrapped its hold on the ground and air surrounding the enclosed yard. His heart became hard and heavy, sinking part of his ribcage as he scrambled to hide behind the stone slab without thinking. In an effort to conceal himself completely, he wrapped his hand on his mouth and nose to avoid any sound, fearing that the shadow was sentient and aware of presences. The other hand was covering pressed against the ground, posed to sprint from his spot, and slowly breathing through his nose to keep silent as possible. He would do his best to sense the environment around him, feeling the earth to see if it'd collapse beneath him. The shadows drew closer; he could make out the emptiness as it approached closer. He held his breath, afraid to make a sound or look behind his shoulder. The crumbling of the earth and dying whispers of sound drew slower and closer to him. It stopped abruptly. The world stood still and silent as it felt only a few inches away from his spot. His heart raced as he prayed with grief and hopelessness, wondering why this kept happening to him.

Nothing, however, seemed to recede or be called off by some force; the damage done was restored as if puzzle pieces were placed back into their spot in reversal. Nemo waited there in disbelief as the Nothing echoed through the night. The sound of the world returning with the buzz of insects, caw of ravens, and swaying wind of the sky. He sat there, hearing all of this, fearing it was a trick to trap him. Nevertheless, he couldn't bear the anxiety any longer. Slowly, he looked up and saw the stars had re-appeared, shining down on him with an ethereal light amongst the moonlight peeking through some clouds briefly. Star-struck, he rose from the clutched spot, looking around his surroundings and then behind him abruptly. His hands clasped the edges of the tombstone like a shield, but he found Nothing or rather, not the darkness but the world in its normality...

Nervously, he gave a snorted laugh in relief, the weight on his shoulders lifting, and began to feel light-headed for a time. For all intended purposes, he had narrowly escaped the literal oblivion. His legs became soft like jelly, buckling in the cold accompanied by a wave of cold sweat beading down his skin. He took the brief time to breathe deeply, kneeling down partially on one knee as he succumbed to exhaustion. At that moment, he felt safe.

"Are you alright, sir?"

"OH GOD, don't kill me!" he screamed.

He spun around and flung his arms, swinging them blindly in front of himself in defense against his unknown assailant with tightly closed eyes. It was cut short once as the figure caught his wrists, causing him to look up to find not another creature or disaster but an ordinary-looking man. He spoke again, maintaining a sincere and calm voice:

"Heh, that's not really in my job description so please, do you need help getting up?"

His grip on Nemo loosen, and for a moment, he hesitated, thinking the worse was still not over. He looked around but still couldn't see any trace of danger. It seemed to be only the man in front of him. He brought herself the courage to answer with a nod, and together, they rose from the ground and stood upright at last.

"Thanks... and sorry, I was being chased by... something earlier," he confessed, looking past his shoulder. He couldn't process what had happened himself and felt he was missing something important. Suffice to say, he couldn't tell him that it was "Nothing."

"Oh wow, I can see why you're on the edge, but I shouldn't be surprised seeing that's been happening for the past few days lately. It's common for pranksters to roam around graveyards and cemeteries in Halloween season. Are you hurt?" he asked, looking around the yard intensely now.

"Yeah, I didn't even realize where I was head- wait... why are YOU here?" he asked, inspecting him up and down.

"Ah, fair question," he coughed nervously, shaking the dirt off his pants with a brush of his hands, "I'm a gravedigger and, no pun intended, here on a graveyard shift. I was just about to finish up when I saw you running in the distance...."

"Oh," he exclaimed and realized by his attire and equipment that he matched the description:

He was an ancient husk of a man plagued with stingy white strands of hair on his elongated, balding head. His face was sagging with pale, wrinkled skin, the bags around his eyes were dug in with a shadow effect, hours spent on the job it seemed. A necklace of keys looped around his collar like an ominous watchdog of the tombs, containing buried secrets of the dead. He had a raggedy, dirt-covered leather coat that was too large for him, stretched over his hunched form as it flapped in the wind. He held his shovel like a crutch, the dark-wooden shaft with a rusted plate resembling a ragged blade. With his callous hands, he rubbed around his chin with his dirt-encrusted nails.

"I'll tell you what," he interrupted as he rubbed the back of his neck, startling her train of thought, "I'm almost done with the shift, I'll walk you back to the entrance. Once we're there and I lock up, you should be safe and can call for a ride home. Sound good?"

"That... that sounds good. Thanks," he sighed, the weight of his fear slowly receding back and the tension in his muscles loosening. Perhaps it was just trauma that drove him to the edge...

Indeed, it felt like he'd be safe at last, and the haunting hunter that was the supernatural would become a figment of his imagination, almost as if it had never existed, so to speak. Together, he made their way through the tombstones and mounds with the old gravedigger, past the mausoleums and statues. All was silent under the moonlit sky. Nemo expected the darkness to charge suddenly at them, but more and more, he searched the ghastly plains. He didn't see anything stirring or any trace of its presence. And thankfully, he could lower his guard and ease the tension in his joints, knowing that the gravedigger would provide some defensive ward; he was at least armed with a weapon and could slow the Nothing down for him to escape faster. It might even be comforting to know that if this was REAL, it could be confirmed, and the misery could be distributed evenly. It wasn't until he stopped abruptly at a grave, causing Nemo to snap back to his senses.

"Sorry, I know we're almost there but I've got to finish up this last addition. It won't take long if you want to wait a bit," the gravedigger suggested, running his fingers across the stone marker and walking around to face the gaping hole.

"Uh, can't it wait until tomorrow? Whatever's out there, it isn't safe for anyone... shouldn't we notify someone, like, right now?" he argued, raising his eyebrow and questioning his judgment.

"I know, but an exposed coffin would only entice scavenger-animals or those pranksters and try to desecrate these corpses. We've already had a case like that before a few days ago..." he glanced at Nemo, nodding his head solemnly, "I understand what you mean through, but it really won't take long."

"Well... I-" Nemo started, not wanting to go without someone, but neither did he wish to stay longer. He stopped when he saw the hole, following the gravedigger around, and side-by-side, he gazed into the massive, deep chasm.

He tried to peer inside deeper, but he couldn't find the bottom, not even an earthy contour hidden in the shadow, as he squinted his eyes. Amazed, he looked at the gravedigger, then back at the hole. He sent a small rock flying straight down the middle of the hole with a kick of his foot. It vanished, and despite perking his ears and listening closely, he didn't even hear an echo behind nor the sound of it hitting bottom. He looked to the immediate right, past the gravedigger, and saw the mountain of scrapped dirt piled onto a substantial blue canvas sheet. It seemed like a lot of work for someone of his size, looking at his rolled sleeves and noting the lean muscle. His eyebrows arched before turning to the gravedigger again:

"That's... um, impressive work, did it take you very long?" he asked, trying to start the conversation to speed up the perception of time and not succumbing to awkward silence. He smirked and shrugged his shoulders but didn't look back at him as he continued his chore:

"This particular family paid extra so I added some extra length and effort but yeah, I had to start earlier than usual...."

"Oh, must've been a big family... how did they die?"

His soft smile had darkened and slowly became more grimace as he rubbed his forehead uncomfortably with a scarlet-red handkerchief pulled from his pocket. He cocked an eyebrow, as if trying to remember, and then lied:

"Couldn't say... but it was a large proceeding, everything was done in order so all that's left is... well, you know."

"Huh, I didn't see anyone else... seems strange only one person did all the work... I can't even see a bottom, are you sure it's down there?" he asked, half-jokingly but curious as well.

"Of course, why would I lie?" he joked, attempting to diffuse the situation.

"Yeah, I guess I'm just... I don't know..." Nemo told herself out loud, "I was always afraid of dying... alone...."

"Love issues, you have a bad break-up and now you're afraid you won't have anyone left in your life?"

"What? Ye-yeah, how did you know?" he asked, perplexed and concerned partially on how he could tell, but more that he didn't understand why he'd say that to a stranger that.

"I get this sixth sense, working with so many people and hearing so many stories, you start to read them easier."

"Oh... I guess that makes some sense."

"I'm not much for love-advice but in terms of 'death,' that comes more naturally given my experience. My advice: you shouldn't concern yourself about dying but try to live your life for more than it's worth. Make it worth remembrance..."

"What do you mean?" he asked, genuinely interested now.

"I mean that death is non-fictional in a sense while life is fictional, you can make it however you want and some people may read into it, but it depends on how much you write and how exciting you make it to be."

"... why a book allegory?"

"I always dreamt of becoming a full-fledged writer in my youth so I can't help it. It just helps conveniently because I felt writing a book is something I could leave behind for years to come. Once I'm dead, and people forget who I am, I can be remembered from what survives...."

"Survives?"

"The books I wrote may survive, and be found in libraries or bookstores, they may collect dust on shelves but there's a tiny chance that someone may stumble on my book. They'll see my name as the author and it'll be imprinted in their memory, even for a brief moment. And that's how I'll be able to live beyond death... I think at least."

"...huh..."

"So it's not dying you should be afraid of but being forgotten, once we are, then you fade into oblivion...."

"That's NOT comforting at all, I feel worse than before," he scoffed nervously, running his fingers through the back of his neck. A familiar sensation ran down his spine, and he wasn't feeling exceptionally safe with this guy anymore.

"How long you think this will take? I can just wait by the gate," he offered, taking an eager step back.

"Not long, and you probably want to stay close. Trust me, it's just pushing the dirt back in. But before I start, can I ask you a question?"

"Uh, sure, but quickly then start burying," he pressed, he was becoming increasingly cold and clammy, and this was putting a foul mood on her; she was considering leaving him behind. And above all else, something just didn't feel right with her...

"I've been writing a short story for Halloween, and I can't seem to find the right ending for this particular character. I want to get it over with and I thought someone could help out," he commented, taking a few steps back quietly without notice.

"Okay, then what's the short-short version?" he asked, focusing on the stone-slab absent-mindedly. He was trying to make out the name, see if it was anyone he knew without paying much thought to the conversation or gravedigger in all.

"Well, after a brutal break-up, the character is nearly killed by a gruesome sea-monster while on the lake, lured into the waters. A day later, he goes to a tavern-bar and finds a n old-fashioned fortune-teller machine that gives him a cryptic message. He leaves and gets chased into a graveyard by a living shadow... Nothingness... UNTIL he comes across an open grave, looks at the stone-marker, and reads his name: Nemo LaNoiré. What should I do with him next?"

He stood there, speechless with a horrified expression on his face as he stared at him with ice in his blood. It was like his jaw was dislocated, hung as he tried to utter any sound, petrified in his place. His body, however, dare not move an inch, but his head turned on its own to face the shrouded grave-marker. It couldn't be true. He'd look at the stone marker and find someone else's name along with the casket below, then he could prove him wrong and leave at once. It had to be so; he couldn't be true, the gravedigger couldn't have known, nor could he be implying his demise. The clouds departed, and moonlight showered them but engraved on the stone:

Nemo LaNoiré
Born on December 25th, 1991
Died on October 31st, 2020
May he be remembered for many years to come,
with the loving memory of those close to him.
God bless his soul.

He read those words over and over again with hot tears streaming across his face like never before. His mind racing to find some resolution or solace. He found none.

"I think," he heard the gravedigger's words drift back, "I'll have him slip on some broken clump of dirt and fall into the grave while trying to escape his fate."

As soon as he heard those words, he wanted to sprint away and tried to do so, turning abruptly, but the ground beneath his heel crumbled as he twisted the turn. He stumbled feet first into the gaping mouth of the grave, and thus, everything began to slow to a crawl like he was floating down. He stared at the gravedigger as he looked downward without any hint of remorse or emotion but still, he reached out.

"But then, he manages to grab onto a nearby root, clinging onto a literal cliffhanger," he continued.

He stopped short, his hand indeed gripped tightly on an upturned tree root, dangling over the abyss. It bore no salvation, and he began clawing his way back, pulling on the dirt madly.

"I wouldn't do that, it'll cause the root to shift and snap soon."

He heard a resounding crack stopped instantly, his eyes widen and frozen, staring at the broken root, barely holding together as it began to strain under his weight. His eyes darted up, and he glared at the gravedigger, only a few feet or a stretched-out arm away from rescue. Accusingly, he bellowed at him:

"Don't just stand there, help me up!"

He merely looked down, bending slightly, both hands resting on the handle of the shovel with his chin nestled between the woven fingers. He ground and bore his clenched teeth as he barked again:

"What the hell is wrong with you? SAVE ME!"

He stood upright, walked in closer, and squatted down as he lowered his shovel down towards him, clasping hard like an anchor to a ship. He couldn't believe his eyes, and he felt that glimmer of hope in him again. Who in their right mind WOULDN'T do the right thing and save him, he thought to himself. Under his breath, he murmured revenge and relaxed slightly, once he was out, he'd be content after he bashed gravedigger's head in with that shovel and leave him to die instead. His fingers were practically touching the blade of the shovel, he could hold onto the backends for support if he lowered it further, but it flew past his palm as he swung it behind his shoulder. It seemed like he was lining up a shot, wielding it like an ax past his head.

"Sorry, but you were planning on "bashing his head in…" anyway," he said.

Nemo held to the root, a loss for words as his entire body felt numb while desperately thinking of something to do or say…

"Not everyone gets a happy ending," he ended, swinging the shovel and severing the root with the blade at last.

Nemo fell backward, screaming only for some brief moments until he was cut off completely, fading into the shadows of the uncertain void, leaving no trace of his existence left. It ended so quickly, and as the moon finally opened up, the clouds dispersing, shined on the graveyard. The moonlight revealed a shallow grave, deep only by six or so feet with a squared bottom. There was nobody left or any sign of a struggle, and so the gravedigger nodded in acceptance.

With that, the gravedigger resumed his duties by filling in the hole with the piles of dirt. Each shovel of the mound was done slowly at his own, relaxed pace. He was almost enraptured in his labor, and all of his senses focused on the task at hand. He didn't stop when he heard another familiar voice creep in, seemingly appearing out of nowhere.

"You couldn't have written a better ending than that?"

"I've re-written so many drafts that I've lost any sympathy for him or anyone else. I just want to finish these stories at last," he grumbled, not looking up and continuing to toil at his work.

"Hm, so what happens next?"

"I fill up the hole, leave the cemetery, lock up the gate, and then hopefully finish the book. With any luck, I'll have written some decent short-stories to scare some readers, and then finally begin my journey as an accomplished author...."

"And if you don't, then you would've done this all for Nothing...."

"... cute," he mumbled, halfway through the pile, "I see what you're getting at...."

"I'm just saying to set your expectations lower, what with all this talk of "happily never after." I'm not implying anything else," she mewed defensively.

The gravedigger rested his shovel on the small, dwindling pile of dirt remaining and shot a dirty look up at her, reaming crouched down with his hands on his knees. With a brush of his sleeve, he wiped the beading cold sweat on his forehead. She simply licked her claws, swiping her paws against her perked ears, still lounging on top of Nemo's oval headstone marker. The cat didn't bother to look back; she laid her head between her arms with her eyes still closed as if asleep, waiting on the gravedigger to be done.

"You know, it's not too late to re-write an ending for you...." the gravedigger mentioned, taking the shovel back and tightly clasping the shaft.

"You wouldn't hurt a poor, defenseless kitten, would you?"

He rolled his eyes; it wasn't worth the effort... or the ink... he thought to himself. Shrugging his shoulders, he threw in the last shovel of dirt into the grave and finished at last. He patted the mound gently and oversaw the end result with a relieving sigh. Standing across the headstone-marker, he examined the engravings as the cat stretched with an arched back, her head to the granite stone. She leaped off and landed on his shoulder, moving to the other shoulder-blade like a perched animal on a pedestal, overlooking the reading of the marker with him.

"You really don't like Christmas, do you?" she asked, tilting her head as she noted Nemo's birthdate.

"I don't HATE Christmas," he interjected, shrugging his shoulders with the cat bracing herself, digging her claws slightly deeper to hold onto him, "I hate people that celebrate it in October, it's a sensible reason I think."

"You COULDN'T think of a different date then?"

"Who cares, do you want a ride back or do you want to walk the rest of the way, Bastet?"

"Yes, please and thank you...."

With a hand clutched at the shovel, using it as an improvised walking cane, he strolled through the walkway of the cemetery while occasionally stroking the neck of Bastet for comfort. Together, they made their way through the gravesite in a somewhat leisurely manner. One by one, they passed each grave-marker until they were only a few minutes to reach the gate again. As they walked, the Nothingness resumed its feast on the world, eating away at the cornerstones of all reality. Piece by piece, the grass-fields... the gray-built structures... the tombs, the grave markers, the mausoleums... the twinkling night sky... the moon... the stars... everything. It was swallowed up into the ever-expanding darkness like pieces to a puzzle board, flung into the empty air. And yet, neither of these characters seemed distressed, the pieces of the ground falling off from each of the gravedigger's steps.

Once they came up to the entrance, everything behind him was turned into a vortex, disappearing into the abyss. The gravedigger set the shovel against the door leading to the caretaker storage unit, a small box with supplies to tend the graves. The wind picked up, blowing the unlocked gates to the graveyard open once more, only to die down in the silent vacuum. The two passed through the archway and started walking down the sidewalk to the adjacent neighborhood. They heard the gates close and lock for the final time on their own. He didn't bother to check, it didn't matter if they were shut closed or not.

"It's almost funny, ironically, I'm scared of the unknown as well..." he spoke unannounced, to Bastet's amazement, thinking he'd be silent for the rest of the night.

"Scared of what's after death or oblivion?" she inquired, resting her head against his shoulder-blade.

"Yes to both, we're all scared of what's lurking in the dark... but for now, I mean I'm scared of what will happen next, once I do get my book printed... will it be any good?"

"Does it matter?"

".... No, I guess not. It'll be my book, and it'll be an achievement in of itself. No one will take it away from me...."

"Then there you go, wake me up when we get there..." she finished lazily, drifting off to sleep.

"If we ever get there, this is the end of the night..." he muttered; he took a few steps forward and stopped in his tracks.

Looking up into the sky, he became enraptured by the stars, the endless starry night as the lights shone brilliantly as the streetlamps and buildings flickered dimly. It was comforting to see the undisturbed shades of purple, blue, and red swirl against each other, little white lights shimmering softly while the moon stayed in orbit, glowing sharply in contrast. His trace was broken by the approaching Nothingness, slowly encircling the two as the rest of the street, the world, as all light, color, mass, and sound was assimilated into the void. Soon, only bits of pavement beneath the gravedigger's feet remained as it crumbled away. Nothing but darkness, no remnants of the world and its living inhabitants. A fine way to end the holiday-season, he thought to himself sadly.

The gravedigger took the only comfort afforded to him, knowing it would be painless as he felt the numbing sensation of the Nothingness entailing his legs like tentacles. Slowly, he left only his torso as he fell into pieces with Bastet still soundly asleep on his shoulders. As a last gesture, he scratched behind her ears one final time as he felt the book begin to close on itself, whispering to the reader:

"Happy Halloween"

END OF OCTOBER

www.ingramcontent.com/pod-product-compliance
Lightning Source LLC
Chambersburg PA
CBHW021015180626
46814CB00003B/1293

* 9 7 9 8 8 9 2 8 5 0 4 0 7 *